Praise for Theolyn Boese's *Daughters of Terra: Book One of The Ta'e'sha Chronicles*

"This is one of the best reads I have had in a long time and like at the end of a perfect meal in a brand new restaurant, I am satiated, but cannot wait to come back for more."

—Louisa Christina, *Erotic Escapades*

"Ms. Boese has written a story that will bring out every emotion. This book leaves you wanting more of this fascinating series."

—Sherry, *Coffee Time Romance*

"Holy hotness, Batman. I think I combusted while reading Theolyn Boese's debut novel. The first book of the *Ta'e'sha Chronicles* series, *Daughters of Terra* knocked my socks off...."

—Francesca Haynes, *Just Erotic Romance Reviews*

"Ms. Boese captured her characters perfectly and in return developed a story that will have you laughing, crying and sighing over the HOT sexy passion that evolves between Theo and her two new husbands."

—Dawn, *Love Romances*

LooseId®

ISBN 10: 1-59632-674-3
ISBN 13: 978-1-59632-674-3
DAUGHTERS OF TERRA: Book One of The Ta'e'sha Chronicles
Copyright © March 2008 by Theolyn Boese
Originally released in e-book format in January 2007

Cover Art by Anne Cain
Cover Design by April Martinez

DISCLAIMER: Many of the acts described in our BDSM/fetish titles can be dangerous. Please do not try any new sexual practice, whether it be fire, rope, or whip play, without the guidance of an experienced practitioner. Neither Loose Id nor its authors will be responsible for any loss, harm, injury or death resulting from use of the information contained in any of its titles.

This book is an original publication of Loose Id. Each individual story herein was previously published in e-book format only by Loose Id and is a work of fiction. Any similarity to actual persons, events or existing locations is entirely coincidental.

Printed in the U.S.A. by
Lightning Source, Inc.
1246 Heil Quaker Blvd
La Vergne TN 37086
www.lightningsource.com

DAUGHTERS OF TERRA

The Ta'e'sha Chronicles, Book One

Theolyn Boese

Dedication

For Steve (Squab!), without whom this book would never have been finished. He was my biggest cheerleader/ass kicker. I needed both. Also, in loving memory of Kimberly Powell, killed by a hit and run driver in July 2006. I miss you, wench.

Prologue

More than eleven thousand years ago...

Ten figures joined hands, heads bowed in supplication. Five perfectly matched pairs, each pair created in shades of gray, red, black, white and aquamarine. Thigh length hair writhed around their bodies as if it had a life of its own. They released hands with their neighbors.

The five women met in the center of the circle they had formed, clasped hands again and raised their voices in a trilling, wordless croon. Their faces were beautiful enough to make the greatest artist weep. Graceful necks smoothed to gently curving shoulders and proudly arched breasts. Perfect hourglass waists flowed into full hips that graduated to the scales of fantastical fish tails. Each woman's body appeared in varying shades of the same colors.

The men moved behind the women with a flick of their own tails. They hovered protectively and rested their hands on the shoulders of the woman in front of them. Their deeper voices added a vibrating rasp that supported the women's lighter tones. Each powerful, masculine form radiated strength and purpose. Wide of chest and narrow of hip, they matched the shading of the woman before them perfectly, as if each pair had been carved from the same gem.

As one, the song ended, their voices stilled.

Moments later they spoke. "Great One, We beseech Thee, hear Us, please." Their voices echoed and twined together.

After a brief pause, Byasuen spoke, "The waters of Earth no longer cradle Our children in comforting arms." Her white hair twined with that of the man behind her.

Kashka continued without pause, "We can no longer protect Our children from war and hatred."

A single tear slid from Iliria's eye. "We can no longer heal Our children's wounds, for the very waters burn them."

"We cannot succor the souls of Our children, they do not wish for rebirth," Shaysha whispered mournfully.

Ecoha squeezed Byasuen's shoulders reassuringly. "Our children's children are born dead or deformed, unable to breathe the polluted waters."

"The human men steal Our daughters, burn away their gills with hot knives so they may not return to the sea and sell them as concubines," Vosh growled out angrily.

Mo'aton rested his forehead on the crown of his mate's head. "Sickness spreads, and with it a despair that cannot be cured."

Solune drew a deep breath. "Our children's souls cry and cannot be comforted, many of Our children take their lives early, in that despair."

As one they spoke again, "Great One, We have failed in the trust You have placed in Us. Do with Us as You will, but, please, take mercy on Our children. Give them refuge; succor them, as We cannot. They are beloved to Us."

Minutes passed in silence. They waited, hoped.

"Ahh, My children…" A sexless voice came from the darkness. It teased and caressed them like a playful wind. "You have not failed Me. Nor have You ever failed Your children. Truly, You would give all, Your very souls, to care for and protect them. Would that all of My children shared Your love." A light glowed in the center of their circle, its colors flowing and changing without pause.

"Gather Your children to You, all that will come. I will see that they are safe, that You may continue to teach and love them. In twelve days You shall have refuge." The voice caressed each of them again and then the light faded.

The ten Gods and Goddesses of the People of The Sea sagged in relief, tears of hope and joy streaming down Their faces. Their children would be safe.

Chapter One

Present day...

Dark eyes stared blankly at the screen showing the never-ending scurry of human life on their pitiful mud ball of a planet. "Filthy beasts. They are so complacent in their own sense of superiority. Everything they touch is infected by their puffed up sense of self worth and then begins to decay. They destroy without thought and feel that everything belongs to them to do with as they see fit. Is this the answer to everyone's prayers? These hairy little monsters?" A malevolent smile graced perfectly formed lips. "I'll make my people understand. We must not let these foul humans infect us as they have everything else they have come in contact with. Our children will not be born of men mating with barely sentient animals!"

* * *

"She's perfect," Kyrin murmured softly, watching the delicate brunette hurry along the sidewalk. "Have you finished logging her yet? I want her brought aboard within the week." He glanced down at the screen that listed all the information gathered about their target. It showed her medical history, career and social life, and list of debts, as well as a catalog of all items in her home.

"Yes, sir. We can bring her in at any time. It's estimated that all of her paperwork can be completed within twenty-four hours of pick up. She does not have any family living, so that's one complication we won't have to deal with this time. The letter of resignation for her place of employment has been prepared, also we have all her outstanding debts and the lease on her apartment ready to be paid," said the tall, slender, man on his left. His pale green hair swished against his back in the long tail he had it bound in as he turned to make a note on his holoreader. "Would you like us to begin the transfer and collection of her belongings? She will be working for the next six hours."

Kyrin nodded thoughtfully, leaning back in his chair. "Yes, bring her in after she finishes work. Start the paperwork and money transactions." He smiled slowly. "I want this one; have her marked as soon as she arrives. Tell the medics I'll be down after the preliminary examination is completed. I'll give them my wishes then."

Whist blinked in surprise. "Of course, sir. I'll begin immediately, and congratulations, sir." He grinned, with a pleased look on his thin face. "Would you like her belongings sent to your quarters after decon, or shall we prepare rooms for her?"

"Expand my quarters into the family set next to mine and place them there. Seal the hall entrance and have one added off the living area. Have her music and entertainment articles downloaded into my computer, but bring her novels. She has an intriguing collection. The living area in the second set of rooms can be converted into a library. Make sure that there are three extra bedrooms available after the addition is completed. I'll be in my office if I am needed."

Standing, he strode gracefully to the door. He paused and turned. "Oh, and Whist? I get half of whatever you won!" Kyrin winked before striding out.

Kyrin was well aware of the betting pool among several members of his staff. It was a common belief that he would not ever mate with a female, but intended to remain with only his lover, Daeshen. His decision to select a female mate would have the entire ship buzzing with gossip within the next few hours.

* * *

Sighing, Kyrin threw himself into his chair and propped his booted feet on the edge of his desk. Rubbing the back of his neck he contemplated the decision he and his lover, Daeshen, had made. His hair flowed smoothly out of the tight braid he kept it in and rippled gently.

"Computer, show subject Conner, Theadora." He studied the image that appeared and rotated slowly over the top of his desk. Her body was delicately muscled with small breasts and full hips. Long, wavy, hair swayed gently to the tops of her thighs. A long fringe of bangs brushed the heavy lashes that framed dark gray, wide set eyes. His fingers itched to touch that hair; would it be as soft as it looked? He had never thought human hair was particularly interesting, despite the comments he'd overheard from some of his mated crew. How could it be that intriguing? It wasn't like his race's hair, which was in fact slender muscles that could move with a thought. Human hair simply hung there. Hers, however, seemed different. It was a deep, rich red-black that glittered with jewel tones in the sunlight. Maybe that's what was so intriguing. He'd never seen hair that shade before. Ta'e'shian hair was rarely so dark.

He eyed the firm, almost stubborn set of her jaw and smiled inwardly. *This one is strong; she'll be able to adjust to her new life.*

He shuddered, thinking about some of the first women who had been taken. Several had tried to kill themselves. The medics had quickly learned to sedate newcomers and implant modified versions of the crew cerebcoms before beginning their procedures.

There were still four women in stasis that could not be allowed to revive. Every time they had awakened they began screaming hysterically the moment they laid eyes on one of his people. Thus far the medics had not been able to pinpoint what the cause of their fear was. All of the women had seemed to accept their new lives easily. Then, suddenly, they began to have unexplained panic attacks. By rights the subliminal messages given to the women when they were first brought aboard the ship should have taken effect long ago and calmed any fears they had.

He regretted the necessity of taking these women. His leaders justified it to themselves by saying that the planet they were being taken from was in danger of being overpopulated. But, then, they were not the ones who had to see the despair, fear and anger that his crew dealt with.

Ten solar years ago a virus struck his home planet. It had spread through the population like a foul wind. Everyone who was exposed sickened from it. Anyone who was already ill, or weakened, died of the fever. Finally, the cause was isolated and a vaccine was found.

It was too late, though.

Soon after it was discovered that the same fever had left the female population barren. The only fertile females left were those who had been off-planet at the time of the outbreak, which was a very small part of their female population.

Their council members immediately ordered a search for a compatible species. It was found in a tiny backward planet known as Earth by its inhabitants. Five ships were dispatched to collect females as mates for the crewmembers and passengers. The unmated female crewmembers were asked to allow their eggs to be harvested during the journey so that they could be donated to the now barren women on Ta'e for in-vitro-fertilization.

It was the council's hope that this would increase the number of full-blooded Ta'e'shian children born. The hospitals on Ta'e were trying to calculate how many eggs were needed and which woman's eggs could go where. The information would be needed when the children reached the age to have children of their own to prevent marriages to people of the same family line.

Leaning forward, Kyrin cleared the floating image and called up what seemed to be a never-ending list of things requiring his attention. *No matter how advanced computers seem to get it never seems to cut down on clerical work.* He grumbled silently to himself.

* * *

Thea glanced quickly down at her watch and noted with relief she only had five minutes to go before she could head home and put her feet up. Juggling the plates in her hands she neatly slid them in front of the two men sitting in a booth. "Can I get you anything else?"

One of the men eyed her and leered. "Yeah, how about your phone number?"

Sighing inwardly, she plastered a smile on her face and rattled off the number to the local animal shelter.

The man's eyes bulged. "Can I borrow your pencil?"

Grinning a bit, she handed it over and repeated the number for him.

Taking her pencil back she wove her way through the tables toward the kitchen and slipped into the backroom to grab her things and clock out for the day. She rolled her shoulders to stretch the muscles before reaching back to untie her apron. Tossing the dirty clothing into the hamper and grabbing her coat and purse, she prepared to make her escape.

"Hey, Thea, taking off?" Sharon, the evening shift waitress, peeked into the room with a friendly smile. She was the classic personification of a truck stop waitress and proud of it. Bleached blonde hair was teased within an inch of its life and a danger to any ceiling fans in the vicinity. Blue eye shadow applied as a solid, glittering, mass across her eyelids and a wad of gum stuck firmly in her teeth completed today's ensemble.

"Yeah, I've got a date with a glass of wine and a Gerard Butler movie." Thea grinned.

"Well, better hurry, the boss is in one of those moods. He's been back in his office humming and combing what's left of his hair. I think he's gonna hit on you again."

Thea groaned and slipped her coat on, edging for the door. Her manager was overweight, balding and convinced he was conceived as a blessing to womankind. He was also convinced that said womankind was far too stupid to understand their good fortune. "You didn't see me leave." She waved her hand in front of Sharon. "These are not the droids you are looking for!"

Sharon giggled softly, watching Thea creep exaggeratedly toward the door. "Nut." She grabbed a couple plates and headed back to the dining room, shaking her head.

Quickly walking the four blocks to her apartment Thea decided what she wanted for dinner. *Tacos sound good, but not exactly wine food. Ahh, what the hell, not like anyone is eating with me who'll care.*

After stepping inside the building she punched the button for the elevator, absently noticing the tall man who came in right behind her. *Rocky road ice cream later, who cares what my hips look like?* She stepped inside the elevator and pressed the button for her floor. The stranger slipped in and stood quietly behind her. Digging in her purse for her keys she did not notice how close he was till he spoke.

"Excuse me, miss."

Looking up, she blinked at the small canister being held in front of her nose. Edging back, she opened her mouth to scream just as a fine mist sprayed her face. Instinctively drawing in a startled breath she stumbled backward, colliding with the wall as her knees gave out. She was aware of his catching her. Dimly, she heard him say something about a subject being captured as her vision blurred and she fell into darkness.

* * *

"Subject captured, Whist. Damn, the captain got himself a pretty one! Is her home cleaned out?" Maren lifted the unconscious woman easily into his arms as he strode from the elevator toward her apartment.

"Yeah, you clear to bring her in?" Whist replied.

"Yes, heading back now."

Maren strode into the apartment and carried the woman to the window, where his transport waited on the balcony. He secured her upright in a cargo web before settling in the chair in front of the controls. Carefully, he activated the transport and edged it up and out of the balcony before heading back to the ship. Once the controls were set he turned and eyed the woman. *We're almost at full capacity now, just a few more women.* He ignored the faint twinge of guilt he felt about ripping these women from their lives. Resolutely, he turned his attention to the controls.

Chapter Two

Kyrin groaned softly and rolled over as his cereb chimed softly again, notifying him that he was needed in medical. Slipping from the bed, he quietly dressed in the dark. A soft grumble came from the bed and he looked up, smiling.

Daeshen opened one sleepy eye and stretched sensually against the silky sheets. "And just where do you think you're going?" His arm snapped out, catching Kyrin's belt and yanking him back down to the bed. Slipping his other hand behind Kyrin's neck Daeshen pulled him down for a soft nibbling kiss.

Humming softly in his throat, Kyrin deepened the kiss for a moment before lifting his head. "She's here, medical just paged me. I'm going to go give them our samples and specs." Watching Daeshen roll onto his stomach, Kyrin slowly trailed his fingers along his lover's spine. He admired the long elegant line of his lover's back. Several heavy strands of Daeshen's silvery blue hair curled around his forearm.

Peeking up from the pillow he was hugging, Daeshen smiled. "I was reading some of the books in her collection… She is very interested in her species' water mythology, isn't she? I found the tales of the merfolk very interesting. She seems to have collected stories from almost every culture on her planet. It will be interesting to discuss it with her; some of them mirror things in our own history. However, I found that rather large collection of erotica even more fascinating." He grinned.

Kyrin grinned back. "As did I. I think she'll be very happy once she settles in." He stood and glided to the door.

Making his way to the medical area he commed Whist. "How many pickups left, Whist?"

"Fifteen, Captain. As well as the twelve passengers left to make selections. I have all our data ready to transmit to the other ships for the remaining subjects who weren't chosen. Also, we have retrieved all the samples we were scheduled to acquire."

"Very good, has the paperwork for Theadora been completed?"

"Yes, Captain. Her belongings have been deconned and will be delivered during the next shift. Her media articles, excluding her books, have been downloaded. She had a rather archaic computer setup, even for this planet's standards. We took the liberty of removing the information and wiping the memory before donating it to a local charity along with the media items. The data was also loaded to your personal computer."

"Thank you, Whist. Carry on." His eyes gleamed as he commed Daeshen. "That charming brat Whist downloaded her computer to ours. Would you care to see if you could find those files she found so very *enthralling?* Having watched her read them, I'm dying of curiosity."

"I would love to." Daeshen's deep voice purred in his ear. He, too, was very curious about those files, considering how aroused Theadora became when she read them.

Kyrin entered the medical area; he paused for a moment, scanning the five unconscious and nude women on the tables before settling his gaze on Theadora. Approaching the table, he inspected her features. She looked so soft and innocent, despite the shapely breasts rising gently with each breath. His gaze slid slowly along her body, pausing for a moment to study the curls adorning her mound before continuing along her legs to her small feet. He blinked and leaned closer to peer at the strange color of her toenails. *Purple?*

"Ahh, Captain, thank you for joining us." Kyrin turned to watch Chief Medic Corvin stroll toward him. "Lovely, isn't she? Her shading is exquisite. I have finished the exam. I'll need your samples to begin the conversion."

Kyrin removed two vials from his pocket. "Here they are. Daeshen's DNA also needs to be imprinted." Inspecting the woman before him again he frowned slightly. "I have some other things I would like changed as well."

The Chief Medic accepted the vials. "Both of you, hmm? Very well." Taking a small stylus and board from his pocket, he made a few notes. "Subject: Conner, Theadora. Subject is in good health, without any medical problems which may prevent conception, no noted diseases or mental imbalances. Her age is twenty-five Terran years, no known living family. It's noted that there is no sign of sexual activity, her hymen is intact. This is very unusual for her culture." He paused to make a few more notes. "She will begin ovulating within the week. That gives us just enough time to convert her genetic structure without destroying the egg." He looked up and smiled. "With luck you and Daeshen could be fathers within the year, Captain. Now, what are your requests and we'll see what we can do?"

Kyrin returned Corvin's smile. "That would truly be a blessing from the *Lithen*, the Gods and Goddesses!" Tilting his head, he eyed Thea, imagining how she would look pregnant. "Please remove her body hair. Place our marks at the base of her throat." He brushed a finger over her pubic hair. "I'd like eight piercings. Four along each side of her labia please. Have her cereb add the sublims for shipboard life as well as the standard cultural information and language. Since she'll be living aboard with us I want to make her transition as easy as possible. Has the symbol for her name been prepared? Daeshen is eager to have proof of our mated status." He grinned happily.

"Very good, sir. Those can be completed before the conversion and will be healed before she is sent to your quarters. I'll check with the artisans regarding her name symbol tomorrow. As soon as it is prepared I'll have them notify you." He frowned thoughtfully. "A problem has come up that I wanted to discuss with you."

Kyrin raised an eyebrow. "What problem?"

Corvin cleared his throat. "We have several passengers and crew who have asked to have extensive surgery done to make their new mates look more Ta'e'shian. It can be done, but is not healthy for the women. The trauma to the body from the surgery weakens them, and the resulting change in appearance will cause panic and a great deal of emotional distress."

Eyes narrowing, Kyrin nodded shortly. "I'll deal with it. Please give me a list of those who have asked. Other than general cosmetic alterations have people speak to me before completing them. These women are not Ta'e'shian and need to be accepted as such. Also, have the crew and passengers psychscanned again. I want you to check for xenophobic behavior, before it's a problem."

The Chief Medic looked relieved. "Thank you, sir. I'll begin the scans today. Your mate should be ready in forty-eight hours. I'll have her delivered to your quarters after the conversion finishes, along with the revival spray."

* * *

Checking his cereb for the time, Kyrin headed back to his quarters. He wanted to get a few more hours of sleep if he could. The last preparations for the trip back home had kept him up late far too often in the last few cycles. *Damned if I'm going to start my mated life off dead tired! She going to be scared enough without having me looking like something the tide left on the beach!*

Daeshen looked up from the computer screen as Kyrin entered and leaned back in his chair. He smiled faintly. "I found the files. Seems our little mate has a few fantasies involving two men and restraints." He rolled his shoulders. "They are science fiction too. Goddess, I'm tired. Can we go back to bed? I'll finish reading these tomorrow." Daeshen stood and padded back to the bedroom.

Kyrin followed him, releasing the closures on his uniform as he went. He quickly stripped and slid into bed, curling his body around Daeshen's. "She'll be delivered in two days. Also, according to the CM she'll be fertile by that time. If the Lithen smile we will begin our family this week." Kyrin nuzzled Daeshen's heavy topaz blue hair, inhaling his scent. "Her possessions will be delivered in the morning; will you be here?"

Daeshen nodded sleepily. "Yes, I made arrangements to work here for the next fifteen cycles after you told me she was being picked up. I'll start setting up her rooms after everything is delivered. I'm sure they just boxed everything up and sent it through. There will be things that should be sent back down." He rolled over to look at Kyrin uncertainly. "Are you sure you want to do this? Once she's converted there's no going back."

Catching Daeshen's wrists and pinning them above his head, Kyrin bit his lover's throat sharply. "You're mine." He lapped the small wound soothingly when his lover twisted slightly in silent protest. "And so is she. We are finally going to have a family, she will be attracted to both of us and with her interests I think she'll settle in easily." His lips trailed lightly down his lover's chest, stopping to swirl lazily around a taut nipple, drawing a gasp from his throat. He smiled around the tightening flesh, enjoying the shivers and gasps from his attentions. His body tightened in interest.

Daeshen's nipple hardened under Kyrin's lips and tongue making him hum happily. Holding his lover's wrists in one hand he stroked slowly down Daeshen's chest with his free hand. He paused for a moment to trail his fingers lightly over the ticklish spot where his leg met his groin.

Daeshen jumped and laughed, wiggling free. "Hey! Quit that!" He rolled onto his knees and stuck his tongue out at Kyrin. "I thought you wanted to sleep."

Kyrin reached out and caught a handful of Daeshen's hair. "We can sleep later, and I want you now. After she wakes we won't have quiet time together for some time, we'll have to focus on her." He tugged gently, pulling his husband-to-be down to his chest. His lips slid firmly across

Daeshen's as his hands stroked a body he was achingly familiar with. Kyrin's tongue teased Daeshen's mouth open. Their tongues danced lightly together.

His lover's body melted against his, fitting them together with the ease of long practice. Daeshen's leg slid between his thighs to rub lightly against the erection hardening there. He swallowed the harsh groan that sounded into his mouth as Daeshen arched against him. Daeshen scooted lower, breaking free to lick his way down Kyrin's chest. Kyrin felt the muscles in his abdomen jumping as Daeshen's tongue swirled erotic patterns across it. The tip of his cock bounced against his lover's chin urgently.

"My… Is this for me?" Daeshen crooned as he lapped the swollen flesh teasingly, and fluttered his lips gently along the series of frills that spiraled down the crown.

Kyrin released Daeshen's hair to fist his cock and stroke it hard and slow from root to tip. "Why yes, I believe it is." He watched a pink tongue dart out and taste the tip again and shuddered. "Gods, I love that." He massaged the base of his dick slowly as those lovely lips pursed over the purple crown and slowly opened, taking it into the moist depths. He groaned at the wet suction. His hands gripped Daeshen's shoulders and massaged the muscles firmly in time to the deep in and out movements. "Oh, yes, just like that…"

Moments passed while sounds of heavy breathing and the scent of male sweat filled the air.

Daeshen released Kyrin's cock with a wet pop and crawled sensually up his chest, pausing here and there for a nibble or kiss. Latching their mouths together for a hot, wet kiss he blindly fumbled for the drawer of the bedside table they kept beside the bed. His fingers slid across the smooth globe of lubricant they kept there and he drew it out. Sitting up to straddle Kyrin's thighs, Daeshen squeezed a dollop of the cool gel into his palm. Tossing the bulb aside he rubbed his hands together to warm the gel before sliding both hands around the up thrust shaft of Kyrin's cock and stroked slowly up and down, spreading the lubricant evenly.

He watched Kyrin groan and raise hips to press his hard flesh eagerly into Daeshen's strong hands. Each pull made shudders rush along the other man's muscular form. Amber brown eyes watched him as Daeshen rose above him and carefully fitted Kyrin's cock to the tight rose of his anus. *He's so beautiful*, he thought to himself, *like a golden statue, only so much warmer.* He reached down to caress the defined muscles of his lover's stomach as he slowly sank down, encasing Kyrin's aching hardness into his tight, welcoming body.

Daeshen shivered as his ass came to rest on Kyrin's pelvis. His hands came up to lace their fingers tightly together as his dark blue eyes opened to lock with Kyrin's fiery amber gaze. He panted softly, savoring the feeling of being penetrated by the man he had loved since they were children. The perfect rightness of the moment brought tears to his eyes as he gazed at his beloved. His hips rose slowly and sank down just as slowly. He gloried in the way Kyrin's eyes darkened and his nostrils flared in response to his slow movements. He prayed that the feeling of rightness would only grow when Theadora joined them in their marriage bed.

He gasped as Kyrin abruptly sat up and neatly flipped them both over, without withdrawing. Daeshen clasped his fingers with Kyrin's again as he gazed intently into the other's eyes. He accepted each slow, hard thrust into his body. "I love you. Always." Daeshen kissed him gently, just the lightest of brushes. His lover hummed with gentle pleasure as Daeshen's strong thighs cradled and wrapped around Kyrin's hips securely.

"And I love you," was the soft reply. Moans followed that soft declaration. Daeshen's cock was caught between their bodies and it was being stroked with each thrust. He lifted his head and bit Daeshen's lip gently.

Kyrin began to move with greater urgency, feeling the increased need to stake his claim on his lover. His hips moved faster, driving harder. His balls drew tight to his body and he gritted his teeth, fighting his impending orgasm, wanting to draw this time out. He shouted harshly when Daeshen suddenly stiffened beneath him and his cock began spraying pearly ropes of cum between their stomachs. Unable to hold back any longer his frills snapped open, locking them together. His semen splashed hotly inside Daeshen.

The men rested together as their orgasms continued for several long moments. They shuddered and shook, holding each other tightly. Finally, they relaxed, exchanging soft kisses and murmured words.

Kyrin gently withdrew from Daeshen's body and slid languidly off the bed. He stretched and smiled, reaching down to pull a sleepy Daeshen up and gently herded him into the bathing area for a quick, hot shower.

He turned the water sprays on to a low setting and slowly washed the other man's body clean.

Kyrin cradled Daeshen against him, feeling boneless with satisfaction and the need for sleep. He rinsed the signs of their passion from Daeshen's body before cleansing himself. "It will only get better, I feel it," he whispered. He stepped from the shower and wiped the water from his body with a warm towel, performing the same action for Daeshen after he shut off the water and stepped out.

Daeshen stole another kiss. "I know."

The men stumbled tiredly back to their bed and quickly fell into a deep sleep, wrapped in each other's arms.

* * *

"Did she save everything she ever owned from the age of five, or does it just look like it?" Kyrin grinned at the frustrated growl from the other room. "And *why* does she own four copies of the same book?" A slight pause in the grumbling followed by a loud thump and a round of lurid swearing. He peeked around the door cautiously. Daeshen's braided tail flicked in short, choppy jerks, a physical manifestation of his irritation, as he rubbed his head and glared at a small metal statue on the floor.

"Sounds like someone skipped lunch again." Kyrin leaned against the wall just inside the room. He looked around, noting that most everything had been unpacked. "You've been busy, how did you manage to get so much out and put away so quickly?" Pushing himself away from the wall he inspected a wall hanging depicting a lovely woman sitting on a rock in a forest combing her long hair. He moved slowly along the wall, admiring the other hangings.

Daeshen blew out a frustrated breath as he turned to glare at his lover. "I had a service unit help." There was a smudge of dust on his nose. Kyrin wisely didn't point it out.

His lover was very particular about his appearance. "You would not believe the things she has! A *felbos'* lair has less junk! Broken shells and badly dyed feathers, books that are falling apart, I think I found a whole nest of animal fur in a box! *Why* she has a box of fur I would like to know!" Throwing his hand in the air he began to pace. "She has photos of rocks, thousands of little paper cards, I think they are to a game. And don't even get me started on the candles! *And not one thing has been dusted in at least a year!* They probably had to overhaul the entire decon unit afterwards!"

Swallowing his snicker when Daeshen turned to glare at him, Kyrin schooled his face into solemn innocence.

"You weren't laughing at me, were you?" Daeshen glowered, stalking toward him.

Eyes widening, Kyrin back up a step. "You have dust on your nose."

Daeshen stopped and made a sound like a kettle boiling over and went off again, scrubbing at his nose, smearing more dust than he removed. "Of course I have dust on my face! Why not, no doubt I'll be added to her collection of bits! But, the first thing she's going to learn is that --"

Kyrin burst out laughing.

Daeshen growled, "This is not funny!"

Calming himself, he looked up. Daeshen's face was coated with dust, making his elegant lover look like a Terren raccoon. He started laughing again. "You missed a spot." He drew in a great gasping breath, trying to stop laughing. It worked until he looked at Daeshen again.

Daeshen glared at his sniggering mate and snarled under his breath, stalking from the room to the cleansing facilities.

"*You* can finish setting up her rooms!" he bellowed, wishing he had a door to slam.

Still muttering under his breath he punched the buttons to fill the huge bathtub in the center of the room. He turned and began jerking off his soiled clothing. He threw them down the laundry chute with another growl and stepped into the shower to quickly scrub before stepping into the now filled and gently steaming tub. Relaxing against the slanted edge he took a deep breath and mumbled the meditation exercises that allowed his lower body to shift. He relaxed even more as his legs joined and formed a scaled tail while his hair loosened and coiled lazily in the water.

A few minutes later he heard the door slide open and opened one eye to a slit. He suppressed a grin at the cautious way Kyrin peered into the room and closed his eye again. There was a soft rustle, a clink and then soft footfalls. Gentle lips brushed his, and a soft caress of love was sent to him along their mental bond. His eyes fluttered open. Kyrin smiled and offered him a glass of pale gold wine. Not saying anything, he sipped the wine and watched Kyrin set towels and his robe in a warmer before turning to pour a handful of salt oil into the water, then push a button to make the water begin to churn gently around him. He smiled as Kyrin silently slipped back out of the room, taking his actions for the apology they were. Sinking deeper into the water he took another sip of wine and let the warm water soothe the tension from his muscles.

Chapter Three

Thea woke slowly. Her head felt like it was stuffed with cotton and ached distantly. Pushing her way through the cobwebs in her brain she licked her dry lips with a tongue that felt too big for her mouth. *Have I been sick?* Every part of her body ached like she'd had the flu. Forcing her gummy eyelids apart she looked around blearily.

She did not recognize what she could see of the dimly lit room. But somehow that did not seem as important as finding something to drink. She tried to sit up, and found she could not move. Her hands were tied together above her head. Memories started rushing back and her body jerked in reaction. The elevator. The man. His spraying something in her face. Her breath came faster as she tried to tug her hands free.

Hearing a soft sound she turned her head and saw a tall, slender man with silvery blue hair walking toward her in the dim light. Pulling harder, she whimpered. *This isn't happening, wake up, Thea!* Her teeth started to chatter as she tried to slide away, only to find her feet were tied firmly far apart. He was almost to the bed now; she twisted harder, sliding against the silky sheets. Freezing, she looked down. *Oh God! I'm naked!* She started bucking wildly, trying to free herself as images of rape and torture started flashing through her mind.

Daeshen ran the last few steps and slid onto the bed on his knees. He slipped his hand over her mouth just before she screamed. "Shhhhh, you're safe," he murmured soothingly, stroking her forehead. She froze under him, eyes opening wide as small whimpers issued from her throat. He sent a brief thought to Kyrin silently. "*She's awake and panicking, I'm going to give her a light sedative.*" Still covering her mouth, he reached over and picked up the small injector the medics had brought with them when they had delivered her. She screamed again when she saw it, cringing as far away from him as she could. Placing it against her neck he pressed the button to release the sedative.

"*On my way,*" Kyrin commed back.

Daeshen watched her eyes, waiting until her breathing slowed and her eyes dilated a bit before removing his hand from her mouth. He gently stroked her hair back, talking to her softly. "You're safe, don't cry." He wiped the small tears leaking from the corners of her eyes away gently. "Would you like some water? You must be thirsty, after being asleep so long."

She nodded jerkily, watching him the way a small animal watches a predator. "Please don't hurt me," she whispered. Trembling, she tried to curl her body into some semblance of modesty, only to be halted by her restraints. A strange lassitude swept over her, warming her limbs.

He placed a small bulb against her lips; water dribbled out. She licked her lips and opened her mouth; more water spilled in. After a few swallows he pulled the bulb away and set it down on a small table beside the bed.

She studied him quietly, briefly wondering why her fear was bleeding away. She knew it was still there, but it seemed far away and out of reach. He looked familiar. Her eyes traced over his face. He had a full mouth and large, dark blue, almost black, eyes. He wore his long hair in a high, tight ponytail that emphasized his high cheekbones. Pale skin stretched over a bone structure of almost feminine delicacy. A dark blue jumpsuit clung to his slender body, showing sleek muscles.

Hearing a whooshing sound she jerked her gaze from his, turning her head to see another man enter the room. She whimpered in her throat again. Slightly shorter, this man had a heavier build. Long roping muscles flowed smoothly under the skin hugging uniform he wore. His long amber brown hair trailed down his back in a neat braid. Cool, light brown eyes studied her for a moment before turning to the other man. Seeing them stand together clicked a memory into place.

Thea crossed her eyes and blinked a few times, trying to focus, but the damned floor didn't seem to want to be still. Maybe that last tequila had been a bad idea. Her friend grinned and waved at her from the dance floor, where she was surrounded by three men vying for her attention. Thea blinked again and swallowed carefully as a wave of dizziness made her stomach grumble irritably. Not gonna barf. Not gonna barf. My stomach is my friend. *She turned and signaled the bartender.*

She asked for a glass of water and smiled weakly when he grinned knowingly at her.

A hand brushed her shoulder while she was explaining to her belly why it should keep its contents. Turning, she blinked up at the man standing behind her. He had long golden brown hair that he wore tied back in a tail at the nape of his neck. Full lips stretched into a confident smile, accentuating high cheekbones and oddly shaped eyes.

Her eyes crossed as she focused on his. Cool. They look like almonds. *She swayed slightly as she leaned forward for a better look at them.*

Slightly up tilted and rounded along the outer edge, they narrowed to delicate points that drew attention to his straight nose. Pretty. *He looked faintly foreign, his features just slightly off from everyone else's. But, in her inebriated state it wasn't anything she could really put her finger on.*

He held out his hand. "Would you care to dance with us?"

Us? *A slightly taller man stepped up behind the first and smiled at her. Just as handsome as the first, he had dark blue eyes and pale, milky skin. She couldn't quite grasp the color of his hair; it looked light, almost silvery. She blinked rapidly as her vision blurred again.* Sex on the hoof, with a side order of omigawd...*she thought to herself.*

"Um, okay." She slipped her hand into his and he led her to the dance floor. She briefly wondered if she was getting herself into more than she could handle. Then she rolled her eyes. Geez, Thea, you've been reading too many serial murder novels. It's just a dance!

She had been tempted to rub against them like a cat in heat and invite them to touch her more intimately. The thought alone had been enough to make her blush and disappear after the song. She had berated herself for leaving so quickly when she got home. Now she wondered if she should have left even sooner.

Thea was jolted from her thoughts by a hand sliding over her collarbone and along the curve of her breast. She looked up nervously. The blue haired man smiled, stroking his thumb over her nipple. He smiled wider when it hardened immediately. Blushing furiously, she looked away, thoroughly embarrassed by her body's response. Chuckling softly he leaned down and brushed his lips along her throat. His tongue traced wet, lacy patterns across her throat and into the curve of her shoulder.

The amber haired man removed his shirt and placed a knee on the bed on her other side. He crawled toward her slowly, the muscles in his shoulders rolling powerfully under his skin with each catlike movement. He smiled darkly at her, sensual shadows rolling across his eyes as he surveyed her helpless body.

She shivered. "Please let me go. I won't tell anyone, just let me go home."

He smiled wider, placing his hand on her jaw to hold her still as he leaned down to kiss her. She moaned softly as his tongue pressed into her mouth for a slow, deep exploration. His grip tightened as she tried to jerk away and he deepened the kiss, twining his tongue around hers lazily. After a long moment he lifted his mouth from her, swirling his tongue slowly along her lips before sitting up.

"Theadora Conner," he spoke quietly, "you are aboard the *Dark Queen*. You were taken to become the bonded mate of Kyrin and Daeshen Auralel." His hand slid along her belly. "I'm Kyrin, this is Daeshen." She jerked under his hand. "Our race needs females to bear our young, and that is the reason you have been brought aboard. Your DNA has been modified to allow fertility with our species. Since Daeshen's and my own DNA was used to make the conversion we are the only males capable of fathering your children. You are now our treasured first wife."

Thea's mind reeled. *Bonded? Bear young?* She blinked rapidly and wondered once again why she was not a screaming ball of hysterics. "B-b-bonded? To both of you? Is that like married?"

Kyrin nodded.

Black laces edged her vision. She struggled to breathe. "I can't be married! I didn't agree!" Looking anywhere but at the two of them. Her eyes were drawn to Kyrin's hand on her belly, then to her hairless mound. "What did you do to me?" she asked shrilly, hysteria edging into her tone, despite whatever they had pumped into her. Raising her head as far as she could she looked closer, every last bit of hair had been removed. "Oh God, this is a bad dream!"

Kyrin's hand slipped lower, his fingers caressing the velvety soft skin just above her slit. Thea writhed under his touch, as her body responded to the soft caress, as well as Daeshen's thumb still stroking her nipple.

Daeshen looked up from his slow exploration of her throat. "Lovely though your curls were we didn't want them; only soft, tasty flesh." He leaned down and lapped slowly at her mouth before taking a kiss, swallowing her soft moan. "Mmmm you taste sweet, and your body agreed before you were ever brought here. That lovely dance aroused you so much we could feel the heat rising from your skin. The change in your scent teased and taunted us long after you left. That was all we needed to know." His mouth trailed slowly down her throat to her breast where his tongue flicked out to trace a fiery circle around her nipple. Moaning softly, he took it into his mouth and suckled slowly.

Thea cried out as each gentle pull drew an answering pulse from her loins.

Kyrin's fingers delved lower, tracing her soft lips. "She's already getting wet." He sucked the moisture from his fingers. "Delicious." Cupping his hand over her mound again, he slid a finger between the lips and slowly stroked her clit. Smiling as she arched into his hand and cried out softly, he slowly circled the moist bud. "We're going to fill this sweet little slit to bursting, darling. You won't leave these quarters until you're mastered and this soft little belly is filled with our child." He smiled into her shocked, wide eyes.

More cream slid from her body as she spasmed at his words. *This isn't right! I can't be enjoying this! What's wrong with me?* Her body seemed to disagree as it writhed on the sheets, straining for more. "No, don't! I don't want this!"

Laughing softly, Daeshen looked up from her breasts. "Yes, you do; those sweet little sounds you're making tell us you do. And, we've read some of your books... Naughty girl." Thea felt blood rush into her cheeks and knew she was blushing. "I'm sure we can accommodate your more, hmm, interesting desires." He caught her right nipple between his thumb and forefinger, pinching it lightly. Taking her left nipple between his lips again he set his teeth around the tender skin and bit. He slowly applied pressure until her back bowed under him. He lapped gently to soothe the sting as her mewling cries rang in the air.

Kyrin slid between her thighs and nibbled small patterns across her hips. "Oh yes, all those nights of watching you read at your computer. Your fingers moving so busily in your little nest." He caught one of the gold rings piercing her lips in his and tugged gently, making her jump. "Now that we know exactly what you want… We'll be sure to give it to you as often as you could possibly desire." His hair unwound from its braid and curled gently around her legs, stroking her soft skin. It slid up along her thighs to curl through and around each ring.

Thea screamed, arching away. She was quickly halted by sharp pain in her tender nether lips as her movement yanked the rings. Trembling, she watched more hair flow over her hips and around her waist, holding her firmly in place. She looked up at Daeshen nervously. "What is that?"

Daeshen grinned as his own hair flowed over his shoulders to snake around the base of her breasts. He nipped her lips. "Our hair is muscle. It responds to our will just like any other." He brushed kisses along her jaw. Daeshen lowered his body alongside hers. He leaned across her. Humming deeply in his throat he rubbed his chest against her breasts. He lapped her throat. Setting his lips firmly he began to suck hard on her skin.

She moaned softly as the strands curling tightly around her breasts squeezed gently, pushing her nipples harder against his chest. Her head tilted back, granting him better access to her throat. A light tugging on her cunt lips caught her attention, making her roll her hips uneasily. Something warm and wet stroked slowly up her slit. Her breath caught in her throat as it danced lightly on her clit. Fire boiled in her veins and she pressed closer, searching for more of the wonderful sensation. A husky chuckle sounded from between her legs.

"Liked that did you?" Kyrin dipped for another taste, lapping up her juices as if they were sweet cream. He lifted himself onto his elbows and she felt his hot gaze moving over her as she writhed below him. Several strands of his hair curled around her clit, stroking it in smooth motions while the strands curling in her rings pulled her lips open further. He slid a finger deep into her body. Her slick muscles contracted tightly around his stroking finger as she absorbed this new sensation. Leaning down again he flicked his tongue along her inner lips. He slowly drew a soft fold into his mouth and suckled gently on the tender bit of skin. His finger twisted slowly inside her, sliding in her slick, hot flesh easily. He slowly pressed another finger into the tight space and gently pumped them in and out. It eased the ache in her core while inflaming her even more.

Thea twisted against her bonds, arching up to meet the delicious sensations of their touch. Her thoughts became even hazier as her body's needs began to overwhelm her. It felt like every nerve in her body was ablaze. The flames seemed to center around her clit, being fed higher with every stroke of the slightly abrasive strands caressing it.

More cream slid from her; she felt it wetting his hand as his fingers stroked faster within her twisting sheath. The molten feeling spread, flowing up her hips and along every inch of her body. Thea felt like she was teetering on the brink of a cliff. She screamed, arching her back, fighting the feelings that were building.

Daeshen raised his head and eyed the dark bruise his mouth left. He smiled with satisfaction. His fingers caught her nipples, petting them slowly and squeezing gently. "That's it, darling, come for us. You look so beautiful." He watched a flush spread across her cheekbones. The bright pink diffused for a moment, then formed faint scrolling patterns. His brows arched in surprise for a moment before his attention was drawn back to the soft, helpless noises his pretty little mate was making. "You look so soft and sweet, all tied up for us to devour. Come, sweetheart, I want to hear you."

He watched as she suddenly arched her back and screamed as her orgasm crested over her. He enjoyed the faintly surprised expression in her passion glazed eyes. Her hips bucked against his husband's hold, and Kyrin quickly slid his fingers from her clenching pussy and plunged his tongue into her sweet sex. Daeshen saw Kyrin's tongue dip into her valley to lap her nectar. Daeshen caught her mouth, thrusting his tongue deep inside so he could swallow her screams and moans. He heard Kyrin humming his pleasure from where he feasted.

She collapsed back onto the bed, panting softly. Her eyes were still glazed from the force of her orgasm. She watched, dazed, as Daeshen slid down her body. He curled up and over her hip and lapped her still throbbing clit. She jerked and moaned softly. Kyrin lifted his head and kissed Daeshen, their tongues tangling together, letting him taste Thea's cream. She watched them kiss, mouths working slowly against each other. Kyrin slid over her other leg, his hair unwinding from her waist, making room for Daeshen between her thighs, who quickly moved into the vacated space and latched his mouth around her seeping slit.

Sucking slowly and hard he drew her taste into his mouth. He pressed his tongue lazily inside her sheath and lapped each drop away, humming contentedly in his throat.

Daeshen felt Kyrin smooth his hair back as his mouth worked avidly on Thea's quivering nether lips. It sent a jolt straight to his groin to know that he was being watched. From the corner of his eye he saw Kyrin reach down to unfastened his pants. The other man drew out his straining cock and lazily stroked himself.

Daeshen rose slowly from Thea's body, licking his lips. "Delicious." He slid from the bed and quickly stripped his clothing off. Catching her ankle, he released the binding, quickly following suit with the other ankle. Pushing Thea's legs apart once again he slid back into place between them. He lifted her thighs over his and leaned forward, kissing her slowly. His tongue danced lightly with hers while his swollen shaft pressed against her still sensitive clit.

Thea moaned softly into his mouth, tasting herself on him. Her body twisted against his. It was like they had crawled into her mind and pulled out all her fantasies. She wanted them to take her, master her, and own her. Her heart and body urged her to submit to them, give them anything they wanted. Her pussy pulsed, aching and empty, eager to be filled. Daeshen lifted off her and sat back on his heels. He rocked his hips slowly, sliding his cock along her lower lips. She looked down, watching him press against her. His cock was thick and long, curving gently up so that the crown rested just below his belly button. The broad flaring hood was covered with slim frills that began at the weeping tip and spiraled down to the heavily veined shaft. At the base of his thick cock shorter hairs waved, curling around the base and along the heavy balls hanging below them. She shuddered with arousal tinged with fear.

"I-I've never done this," she stammered softly, nervously twisting her hips.

Thea whimpered when Kyrin released his cock and reached between her legs to grasp one of the rings piercing her flushed lips. "We know, darling. It's going to hurt, but you'll enjoy that too, won't you?" She panted softly, nervously, as he gently pulled her lips open, preparing her for the next act in this erotic drama. "I promise you'll like it. I know I will."

Daeshen smiled, leaning forward to press the tip of his cock against the small, tight opening of her body. Slowly he pressed inside, listening to her soft gasps as he stretched her untried flesh. He continued to slide until he met a thin barrier. Pausing, he rubbed his thumb over her clit. He held her hips still as she bucked in response. "Mmmm she's slick and tight, Ky." Suddenly he jerked his hips, ripping the membrane and burrowing deep into her body, making her cry out sharply. He closed his eyes against the sensation of her slick sheath writhing along his cock. Taking a deep breath he opened his eyes again. He watched Thea's head roll fretfully against the pillow as her pussy twitched and spasmed, trying to adjust to the sudden invasion. He withdrew slightly and pressed slowly back in. "Ahh, lovely..."

Daeshen moaned deep in his throat, withdrawing almost completely only to surge back in. Holding himself deep he rolled his hips in a slow circle. The waving hair at the base of his cock curled around her bare mound, lightly petting her throbbing clit. His frills trembled inside her, wanting to flare open and hold her in place for his sperm to drench her. Gritting his teeth, he fought back his impending orgasm, determined that she would enjoy her first mating. Shoulders shaking with the effort he pulled slowly from her clinging nest and eased back in. He gently increased the speed of his thrusts, watching her face.

Thea whimpered softly, arching her head back into the pillow. She tried to twist away from the sting; it felt like a burning hot knife was spearing her. Her sex was stretched painfully tight around him. "Oh, it hurts! Please stop, take it out!"

Kyrin leaned over and caught her nipple in his mouth distracted her from the uncomfortable fullness of her sex. He released her ring and cupped the other breast, massaging it gently.

She gasped as his suckling flooded her body with heat. It confused the pain with pleasure and brought her back off the bed. "Oh God!" Her fists clenched above her. Another burst of moisture dampened Daeshen's cock.

Thea bit her lip. Each thrust eased the sting a bit more. The twisting caresses along her clit made her suck in ragged gasps of air. Her cunt rippled lightly along his cock as it moved slick and hot inside her, building the flames again. The frills that spiraled along his cock rasped along her sensitive walls. The sensation was deliciously stimulating. She looked down her body. Her breath caught again at the undeniably erotic sight of Kyrin's cheeks hollowing with each pull on her breast. Following the line of her body she moaned as she watched Daeshen continue his slow measured thrusts into her welcoming body. Each slow withdrawal and insurgence was pushing her closer to that edge again.

Kyrin sat up and leaned toward Daeshen. He curled his hand around Daeshen's neck and pressed their lips together.

Daeshen moaned as his hands curled around Thea's thighs, holding them tightly against him. He opened his mouth to Kyrin's questing tongue. His eyes fluttered closed and he gave himself up to the luscious sensations of his mates' bodies. Curling his tongue around Kyrin's he thrust harder and faster into Thea.

He was drawn sharply back to the task at hand as Thea's hot channel twisted around him. Her back arched sharply as her body was racked by the waves of her orgasm. A keening cry echoed in the air as she clenched tightly around his shaft, contracting and squeezing him with her orgasm.

Daeshen gasped, pressing into her silky, shimmering sheath in quick hard thrusts. His frills flared open, pinning his cock inside her. He writhed as his seed burst, drenching her sucking, milking pussy. He shuddered, leaning forward into Kyrin's supporting arms as she continued to pull at his cock, wringing soft gasping cries from his mouth.

Gradually his cock slowed its frantic jetting into her. His frills vibrated gently inside her, forcing his sperm to stay near the mouth of her womb. It took several minutes before his frills lay down again.

Panting, he pulled himself from her body as his cock softened and his frills relaxed. He collapsed beside her on the bed. Opening his eyes he watched Kyrin caress her body soothingly as she twitched and moaned softly. He smiled, feeling lazy and sated. Stretching, he rolled onto his side and stroked her gently as well. Feathering soft kisses along her jaw he whispered compliments. "You were wonderful, darling. So soft and warm and welcoming." He lapped her lips.

Blindly, she turned her face into his kiss. Gentle pulses swept her body in the aftermath of her orgasm. Opening her mouth submissively, she caressed his tongue with hers, soaking up his compliments and affection. Feeling wrung out and blurry she didn't resist when Kyrin rolled her onto her belly. Soft murmured commands and gentle hands urged her onto her knees. She breathed slowly, feeling herself sink back into her body. Callused hands rubbed over her upturned ass, jolting her back to reality. Jerking free, she started to slide back down. A harsh slap brought her head up.

"Ass up, love. It's my turn."

She quickly brought her ass up as another stinging slap spread fire across her cheeks. Looking back, she saw Kyrin kneeling behind her. His hands slid down the back of her thighs and curled inside, forcing them apart. Thea bit her lip and trembled.

Kyrin scooted closer, sliding his hands over the warm red splotches that were beginning to bloom across the loveliest pair of cheeks he'd seen in ages. "Perfect, I can't wait to spank these." He smiled faintly as a tremor went through her. He grasped his weeping cock and teased it along her slit. "Mmmm nice, wet and oozing Daeshen's cum." Slowly he pressed inside, watching Daeshen's semen pool around his cock.

He watched Thea hide her face in the pillow as he came to rest against her ass. His cock filled the tight space; it was hot and moist around him. Her head came up as he smacked her ass again. Hot red marks bloomed and spread across her fair skin. Another smack, he heard her suck in a gasp of air. Her hips jerked and ground back against him reflexively. *Smack!* She moaned softly and contracted around him. Kyrin spanked her with a quick flurry of slaps that had her screaming and bucking. Just as suddenly he stopped. He listened to her quick pants of relief and rubbed his warm palm over her burning skin

Kyrin purred softly and ground his cock in her, rubbing his belly on her ass. The heat emanating from her cheeks was intoxicating. Slowly he began to piston in her tight little cunt. Soft sucking sounds with each withdrawal were followed by even softer moans with each return. Knowing that he was not going to last long he curled his hand under her belly and pinched her clit.

Thea bucked back onto his cock as she felt him pinch her clit between thumb and forefinger, then began to stroke it in time with his thrusts. The warm glow of her ass spread throughout her sex, making her dew his cock with more moisture. She was rewarded with a deep rumbling growl and the heavy pistoning picked up in speed. His belly slapped her ass, spanking her all over again. She screamed sharply as her body shuddered and writhed back to meet his. Her orgasm swept over her, sudden and overwhelming. Dimly she heard his triumphant roar. She felt something pop inside her sheath again as his cum shot and pulsed inside her.

She felt Kyrin grind himself against her. He was sucking huge drafts of air between his teeth as she stroked his cock with her reflexive motions. Her wet grasping sex felt as if it were trying to suck every last drop from him. He fell forward onto his arms, covering her body and waiting for his frills to retract again. She shivered as he nibbled on her bowed neck. A deep-throated hum vibrated along her neck. He withdrew slowly, drawing a moan from her as his retracted frills scraped along her swollen walls.

Tears streaming down her face, Thea collapsed slowly onto the bed.

As one, Daeshen and Kyrin rolled against her, cradling her sore body between them. They murmured softly and stroked her. Someone reached up and released her wrists. Her arms were pulled down and they massaged the stiffness from her shoulders. Exhausted, she closed her eyes and let them play with her body. Gradually their caresses lulled her. She fell asleep pressed tightly between them.

Chapter Four

Thea woke with her body on fire. A tongue was lapping wet circles around her nipples while a hand was rubbing slowly around her clit. She gasped softly and arched. The hand left her clit and turned her on her side. Two bodies pressed against her. A hand slid between her thighs, lifting her left leg over a lean male hip. She opened her eyes just as Daeshen caught her mouth in a fierce kiss.

Daeshen pressed his tongue into her mouth as his hard cock slid deep into her cunt. He rocked his hips tightly against hers. His hand slid over her hip and grasped her ass, pressing her hips hard to his.

Thea pulled her head back and sucked in a breath as he began thrusting heavily into her. She felt Kyrin's arm slide around her waist, holding her firmly still, making her unable to do anything but accept Daeshen's body in hers. Her head swam in a passionate blur. The pressure of him inside her made her clit swell and send shocks directly to her brain. She wallowed in the rising tide of her orgasm, teetering on the edge.

Daeshen let out a harsh shout and pulsed deep inside her, splashing his cum along her inner walls. His frills flared and stroked inside her with each pulse.

Thea cried out softly, feeling herself slide into orgasm. A sharp slap on her ass jerked her back from the edge. Her breath hissed between her teeth and she writhed at the sudden sting as it yanked her back.

Daeshen pulled free of her body, lifting her thigh. He pressed a kiss to her mouth and reached down to guide Kyrin's cock to her.

Kyrin slid slowly into her. He adjusted his grip on her waist and began to thrust hard and fast. He bit the nape of her neck and cupped her breast, teasing the taut nipple.

Thea moaned, his thrusts pushing her back to the edge of orgasm. She pressed her ass into his abdomen and rolled her hips. "Oh, faster!" She felt his answering moan against her neck as he picked up the pace. Each jolt bounced her nipple between his fingers. Her thwarted orgasm came boiling back up and hung over her like a heavy cloak. She screamed as his fingers pinched her nipple tightly. Stars burst behind her closed eyes as her hips bucked hard against him. She wailed and thrashed against him as her pussy shuddered along his shaft, wringing a hoarse groan from him.

Kyrin's frills snapped open and thick hot sprays of spunk jetted into her. Each time she bucked it drove him a little deeper and locked him higher inside her. He threw his arm over her hips, holding her still as her cries sounded in his ears. "Ahh, Goddess... She's so slick and tight!" He held her tightly against him as he panted softly into her hair. His hand rubbed lazy circles over her hip. Grunting softly, his frills folded back down and he slowly withdrew from her, drawing a soft moan from her throat. He pressed a gentle kiss against the back of her neck.

Rolling onto his back Kyrin stretched slowly. He yawned. Checking his cereb, he groaned. He had fifteen messages waiting for him. Pushing himself out of the bed he padded across the room to check them. Too bad he would not get a vacation until they reached home. Most of the time he was lucky to have a free day. Quickly scanning his messages, Kyrin sent responses for some, and commed others to set up meetings. A soft touch on his shoulder made him look up a few moments later.

"I'm taking Thea to the bath. Join us when you're finished." Daeshen dropped a light kiss on his lips.

Kyrin nodded. "We should probably dose her again. I'd like to keep her calm. We can stop after a day or so and see how she's handling things." He turned back to the computer. "I'll have a crewman send breakfast, it should be here in an hour. What do you want?" He answered another message while he waited.

"Oh, anything, I'm starved." Daeshen swept Thea's hair off her neck. He quickly pressed the injector and administered the dose before she could protest. Frowning, he looked into her eyes, slightly concerned at the blankness in them. "I think you're right about the sedative, she looks a bit shocky. Poor baby." He pressed a tender kiss to her brow. Sweeping her up, he stood and cradled her in his arms. "Let's get you in a nice warm bath, hmm?"

Thea blinked up at him. Her body began to feel heavy and warm again. *Sedative? Oh, so that's why I feel so weird...* She tiredly reached up and patted his cheek. "Sleepy." Her voice was faintly slurred. Her head felt too heavy to hold up any longer so she rested it against his shoulder. She let everything that had happened roll through her brain, digesting it. *I'm living a bad sci-fi novel. With bondage.* Thinking about it, she was actually glad for the sedative. It was keeping things distant enough to allow her time to absorb it. *I'm married to two incredibly handsome men who look like they just walked out of a Japanese anime... Must have been a hentai anime...* She sighed deeply.

Daeshen set her down on a stool and ran a bath. She felt his gaze on her as he watched her carefully. He quickly set out towels. Picking up three bottles he crouched in front of her and opened them. "These are salt oils, darling. Which one do you like?" He offered her the bottles.

Woozily, she leaned over to smell the first bottle. She quickly blinked her eyes as a heavy musk scent assaulted her nose. "Uhhhh." Pushing it away, she sniffed the second bottle. *Why is he being so nice?* It smelled a bit like cedar and cinnamon. "'S one's better." Blinking owlishly she moved to the last one. "Ohhh." It was a light citrus, a bit like lime and grapefruit mixed together. "That one, please." She leaned back and watched him pour a small handful of pale green crystals into the rising water. The fragrance soon filled the room. Dazed, she watched the steam rise and swirl.

The tub dominated the room. It was a huge sunken affair made of a pale gold stone. Polished smooth and curving into a large oval, it was easily ten feet long and at least six feet wide. Water gushed in from three large holes carved into the stone. The rest of the room was decorated in similar colors of paler gold and an even paler cream.

Thick, plush area rugs were strewn around it. A large open shower was set into one wall. A small lip of tile ran along the floor in front of it to prevent water from covering the whole floor. There were doors and closets built along the walls, with knobs made of the same gold stone as the tub.

Thea waited until Daeshen looked at her and smiled tentatively. "This is a beautiful room." She pronounced each word carefully. Shifting slightly on the stool, she winced at the aches in her body. She shook her head when he smiled blindingly at her. *He really is gorgeous...* He crouched in front of her again. *And very naked.* She held her breath nervously when he reached toward her, only to release it in a rush when he did nothing more than brush her hair behind her ear.

Daeshen scooped her up and strode to the tub, carefully stepping down the wide shallow stairs. The hot water swirled around his waist as he made his way to the benches that lined one end. He slowly lowered Thea until the water covered her shoulders and she rested on the bench. He slid down next to her and stretched out with a sigh of contentment. Turning his head along the edge of the tub he regarded his tense little mate. "Relax, love, let the water do its work." Rolling his face back up, he closed his eyes and let his hair wave in the water.

It floated in the water, occasionally brushing along Thea's breasts and waist. He shivered, enjoying the stolen caresses that she probably was not paying attention to. His mind reached carefully for hers, trying to form a bond. Some humans were completely closed to his race, while others could communicate at various levels. He was hoping to at least be able to sense her emotions.

The heaviness in her body was lessening and thought was becoming a little easier as the initial wooziness of the sedative evened out. She looked at the slender man lounging beside her. Seeing his eyes were closed she relaxed against the tub and watched his hair sway against her.

Remembering how it moved over her on its own she eyed it curiously. She reached out to touch a strand and gasped softly as it curled around her finger. Darting a quick look at Daeshen, she saw his eyes were still closed. Looking back down, she rubbed her thumb along the strand; it responded by tickling her palm. Smiling, she leaned closer and continued her inspection. It was about the thickness of her embroidery floss and faintly abrasive. It reminded her of the anemones she had touched at an aquarium on the Oregon coast. The sheer foreignness of the moment cascaded through her brain again making her breathing become harsh. She closed her eyes and reached for calm again. *Just breathe, Thea. Just breathe.*

Several more strands joined the first, curling around her fingers and wrist. She darted another glance at Daeshen. His eyes were still closed but he was smiling now. Letting her hand rest in her lap she scooted down into the water a bit more. She let her legs part a bit so the warm water could wash over the sorest part of her body. She hissed softly at the sting.

Daeshen felt a surge of satisfaction as she relaxed next to him and started to play with his hair. He suppressed a shiver. Maybe one of these days he'd tell her he could feel those feather light touches just as well as if they had been on any other part of his body. His questing mind finally latched on to hers. Slowly and lightly he eased his way in. Her thoughts felt heavy and syrupy because of the sedative, but he was surprised at how calm she really was. Her thought processes felt different from those of his people. Just slightly off, it was like wearing spectacles made for another person. It took him several moments to understand the differences and sort out the meaning. She was trying to accept everything that they had told her and had happened to her. The sheer amount of information was overwhelming, though, so she constantly had to take small breaks as panic and fear created brief, jagged, spikes in her thought patterns. He resisted the urge to send her the surge of pride he felt. Gently, he slid back out of her mind.

Thea's eyes were closed as she continued to run her fingers along the hair curled around her wrist. Something tweaked a nipple. Her eyes shot open and she looked down. His hair continued to wave and sway innocently. She shot him a suspicious look but his eyes were still closed and his expression tranquil. After a moment she closed her eyes again and relaxed. Her mind drifted as the water eased her muscles.

Hearing the door slide open she bolted upright and slapped her arms over her breasts. She saw Daeshen wince from the corner of her eye as she jerked his hair.

She watched with wide eyes as Kyrin stalked into the room. Not bothering with the steps he slid into the water and flopped down on her other side with a sigh. Thea watched him settle in nervously, remembering the spanking from last night. When he did nothing but stretch out and close his eyes she slowly relaxed again.

Kyrin sent a warm tendril of thought toward Daeshen. *"How is she?"*

"She's taking it in, a little bit at a time. All things considered, she's doing wonderfully. I managed to catch a

few stray thoughts, but the sedative makes it difficult," he sent back.

Thea looked around slowly. She saw a small shelf carved into the stone. It held a sponge and bottle of something. Turning her eyes back to Kyrin she eyed him. His large, muscled body floated just under the water. She'd have to reach over him if she wanted the sponge. She chewed on her lip. The desire to wash warred with the possibility of touching him. Daeshen seemed much more approachable.

Feeling her eyes on him Kyrin opened his and looked at her. He smiled tenderly. She was gnawing on her lower lip and eyeing him like he was going to bite her. Reaching up he caught her lip with his thumb, tugging it out from between her teeth. "You should be nicer to such a tender morsel, Theadora. Like this." Curling his fingers around her neck he drew her down to him, suppressing a grin as her eyes kept getting wider. He gently stroked his tongue over her lip. Teasing her lips open, he dipped inside and kissed her with lazy desire. Pulling her closer he deepened the kiss, exploring her mouth until she moaned softly. Releasing her, he closed his eyes and relaxed again.

A soft touch on his shoulder made him open his eyes and look at her. "Yes?"

She licked her lips nervously. "My -- my friends call me Thea." His slow sexy smile almost made her eyes cross.

"Ahhh... But, we aren't friends, Theadora," he purred as he sat up.

She wilted.

He curled his arm around her waist and tugged her into his lap. Ignoring her soft squeak he kissed her again.

Working his way along her jaw, he rumbled in her ear, "We're mates."

Thea curled her hands around his arm reflexively and blinked at a grinning Daeshen. She shivered as Kyrin's mouth feathered delicately along her collarbone. "Oh." Watching Daeshen sit up and scoot closer to them she wiggled in Kyrin's lap, trying to slide off. "Um." She stilled when his arms tightened. *Well, that didn't work out quite the way I expected.* She tentatively wrapped her arms around his shoulders. She had a pretty good idea where this was going and knew she wasn't going to get out of it. The knowledge that she was helpless to escape sent a warm curl of arousal through her, making her blush. *I'm liking this way too much...* She gasped as Daeshen cupped her breast and kneaded it gently.

Kyrin caught her hair and pulled her head back to stare into her eyes. "You belong to us. And we belong to you."

She blinked in surprise.

He caressed her cheek gently. His cock rose and pressed against her buttocks. Smiling wickedly he turned her in his arms until she was straddling his lap, facing him. Reaching between her thighs he found her already wet. "Mmmm, naughty girl, you do like it when we take control, don't you?" He grinned when she blushed a fiery shade of red. Lifting her hips he pressed her against his chest and slowly impaled her on his standing cock. He hummed when her ass settled on his thighs. Her soft gasps echoed in the room. Twisting to the side he grabbed the small bottle on the shelf and tossed Daeshen the sponge, who caught it deftly and moved behind her.

Kyrin poured some of the thin blue gel into his hand before giving Daeshen the bottle. He rubbed his palms together, warming and lathering the soap. He slid his hands up her delicate arms, over her shoulders and down her breasts. He grinned at the soft choking noise he got from swiping her nipples so quickly.

Taking her hands from his chest he massaged the soap into her hands before putting them back and working his way up her arms. When he reached her shoulders he stopped and rolled his hips slowly, making her sob softly at the sensation. Looking over her shoulder he saw Daeshen begin to rub the soapy sponge along her back. She shivered along his cock. Leaning forward to catch her mouth, he kissed her deeply as his hands cupped her breasts and began to knead them in his soapy hands. The small strands of hair at the base of his cock tickled and petted the hard little nub at the top of her slit.

Thea moaned softly, arching her breasts into his hands. Her head touched Daeshen's shoulder and she snuggled into the curve of his neck. Daeshen rubbed the sponge in slow circles around her hips and across her belly. Their tender washing hands unraveled her defenses faster than anything else could. Both of them felt so right. She lifted her arms back behind Daeshen's neck and gave herself up to them. Turning her head she begged him to kiss her in a soft voice.

With a soft growl Daeshen took her mouth in a voracious kiss. She sighed into his mouth as his tongue tangled and danced against hers. Thea enjoyed the sensation of his hands moving in caressing strokes over her legs as he continued to gently wash her. Gasps erupted from her throat as he dropped the sponge to stroke the juncture of her thighs where her body joined with Kyrin's.

Suddenly her mouth was torn free of Daeshen's as Kyrin slipped off the bench and onto his knees in the water. He wrapped his arms under her hips to hold her as he began to plunge in and out of her body slowly. Soft cries escaped her throat as she was bounced on his lap, each insertion a deep, hard prod. Thea dug her nails into his shoulders as she felt tension build in her loins. She felt Daeshen's lips slide across hers as he stole another kiss. His soap slicked fingers slid easily over her bouncing breasts, leaving a trail of heat in their wake.

Thea pulled her mouth away and drew a shuddering breath as her body exploded into a million pieces. She felt that strange popping sensation in her vagina again, just before Kyrin began to pulse. Daeshen pressed her forward into Kyrin's chest and she lay against him and panted. Her body seemed to be trying to milk every drop of cream from him. She felt him slip back onto the edge of the bench as he cradled her tenderly, pressing soft kisses onto her mouth as his cock slowly softened.

At last Kyrin lifted her tired body off him.

Daeshen pulled her close, pressing his erection against her belly. His lips feathered along hers. He backed her into the wall of the tub and lifted her onto the lip.

She looked up at him with dazed eyes as he pressed between her legs for another kiss, splaying her legs around his hips. She lapped his mouth before teasing her tongue between his lips. Her tongue delicately tasted his, becoming familiar with his unique flavor. Her inner muscles clenched emptily. She wanted him, hard inside her. Filling the aching void left by her quick orgasm.

Thea pulled her mouth free and looked up at him. Her hands stroked up the slim column of his chest, pausing to caress his nipples before continuing to absorb the textures of his skin. Her legs curled around his hips and she rubbed her aching core along his throbbing erection. It separated her cum slick lips and the frills at the crown rasped delightfully along her clit. She moaned softly and repeated the action.

He hummed softly and stared down at her with heavy lidded eyes. He stole another kiss and whispered against her lips, "What do you want, love?" A smooth motion stroked her with his erection again. "Is this what you want?" He nipped her lower lip and sucked it into his mouth for a moment. "If you want it you should take it. Show me what you want."

Thea squeaked softly and blushed.

Daeshen smiled and stroked her back. "Show me, please. Show me where you want me…"

She blushed harder and shook her head.

"Oh yes, show me." He pushed her damp hair away from her face and kissed her again. "Lie back and show me your valley. Please?" More coaxing kisses. His hands caressed hers reassuringly.

Still blushing, Thea leaned away from him and drew up her legs slightly. Her trembling fingers reached between their bodies and brushed against where he was pressed tightly against her slick flesh. "Here," she whispered in a nearly inaudible voice.

He smiled and adjusted hips, pressing the tip of his cock against the wet opening of her body. "Here?"

She sighed softly and nodded slowly, looking up into his eyes. "Yes." Her calves rubbed lightly against his hips as she rolled her hips up to him. She was acutely aware of Kyrin watching them from the water. Shivers rolled through her body drawing her nipples into even tighter nubs. She gasped softly as Daeshen began to press slowly inside, separating the walls of her tunnel.

As she watched his eyes glazed and his body came against hers. He paused and closed his eyes and breathed deeply. She curled her arms around him and drew him down to her until their lips met. As she tentatively kissed him it struck her that he seemed familiar to her, as if he was where he was supposed to be, deep inside her. Her heart clenched.

Daeshen moaned into her mouth and began to slowly, lazily, thrust in and out of her willing body. He had never felt this way with another woman. Only Kyrin had ever given him the feeling of freedom he had now. Her lips tasted of fresh water and warm breezes. He was vaguely aware of Kyrin approaching them and caressing Thea.

He listened to her moan as Kyrin's hand stroked over her breast lightly. Daeshen moved faster inside her, making her body rock against the lip of the tub where she sat. She tore her mouth free of his and turned blindly toward Kyrin, who pressed his lips against hers and hummed softly. Her whole body shuddered as she reacted to the sounds issuing from Kyrin's throat.

Daeshen leaned back to give Kyrin room but did not slow his urgent movements. He loved watching them moving together, their tongues twining with each other, the slow forming of bonds among the three of them. He smiled as Thea's hips began to move urgently with his and her slick sheath tightened around him.

Daeshen swallowed her cries and pressed harder against her body as she twisted urgently against him. Her nails dug into his arms, leaving deep stinging impressions. He felt her shivers begin at her core and they quickly swept up to engulf him.

Daeshen moaned and ground himself tightly against her as the sensation trembled up his cock and brought him to a hard fast release. His frills snapped open and cum shot deeply into her, coating her inner body. His hips jerked rhythmically against her as he continued to feel her writhing against him. Daeshen collapsed over her and panted. "Oh Goddess, that almost killed me…" He shuddered again and breathed into her damp hair, listening to her harsh breath in his ear. He smiled and pressed a kiss against her jaw.

Easing away from her he caught the sponge as it floated by in the wavy water. His frills had not yet released. He began rinsing the sticky soap from her skin. After he finished he quickly splashed water on his chest. Pulling Thea up against his chest again he dipped the sponge in the water and squeezed it over her breasts. Finally his penis slipped free of her body. He shuddered at the sensation.

Sliding back in the water he looked around for the bottle of gel. Finding it he raised the sponge to Kyrin with an inquiring look.

The other man turned and presented his back to Daeshen. Daeshen felt him relax into the slow, soft touch of the soapy sponge sliding along his back and shoulders. "That feels good." He rolled his shoulders forward and stretched his neck. Daeshen had to smile. Kyrin loved to be petted and stroked.

Thea watched them with wide eyes. She had never seen two men so comfortable with each other. She blinked when Kyrin stood, the water rolling off his powerful body. Her eyes were drawn to his manhood. It hung heavily against his thighs like a sleepy snake. Looking up at his face quickly she squeaked when he winked at her. Blushing furiously, she looked down at her lap.

The men continued to bathe each other, stealing light kisses and caresses while Thea watched them covertly from under her lashes. After rinsing the soap off they relaxed back in the water. Daeshen gave Thea the soap and sponge before he closed his eyes and stretched out again. "Go ahead and finish washing, love. Breakfast should be here soon."

She frowned down at the bottle in her hand. "Um. Do you have any shampoo and conditioner?" Slipping to the other end of the tub she poured some gel onto the sponge. Scrubbing her legs, she tried to keep as much of her body under water as she could.

Kyrin opened his eyes and frowned at her. "Any what?" Watching her he had to suppress a chuckle. She was wiggling and contorting as she tried to stay under the cover of water and wash at the same time.

Thea squeaked as she lost her balance and slipped under the water. She came up sputtering and swiped the water from her eyes. "Shampoo and conditioner. For my hair?"

The men exchanged a perplexed look.

"It's a special kind of soap and detangler for human hair."

The confusion cleared on Daeshen's face. "Oh, that's what those bottles were for."

Thea blinked. *What bottles?*

Standing, Daeshen waded to the wall curving along one side of the huge tub. He reached for a sliding door between the shower and tub that she hadn't noticed before. After taking two familiar bottles from it he slid it closed again. Making his way back to Thea he offered her the bottles and sat down next to her with a curious look on his face.

Thea wondered briefly why he had her favorite brand. She quickly poured a portion of the shampoo into her palm and worked it through her hair. It foamed up quickly and the scent of strawberries filled the air. Catching the odd expressions on both male faces she froze. "What?"

Daeshen leaned forward and sniffed. "That smells good, what is it?"

She tilted her head and started scrubbing again. "Um, strawberries. Would you like to try some?" Taking a frothy hand from her hair she offered him the bottle.

Curious, he nodded and took the bottle. Mimicking her, he poured some in his hand and began to scrub his scalp. His hair curled up on his head in a pile like hers. Pausing for a moment he thought about the sensation. It felt good. The strands of his hair slid silkily in the shampoo. "Oh, this is nice. We'll have to make more of this. Does it come in other scents?" Normally, he just poured some soap in his hair and let it rub itself clean. He hadn't realized how nice it felt it massage his scalp.

Thea nodded slowly. "There are tons of different kinds of shampoo and conditioners. You probably don't want to try the conditioner, though." She dunked under the water and shook her head to rinse.

Daeshen mimicked her motion, then watched as she smoothed some conditioner into her long hair and combed her fingers through it.

Daeshen slipped behind Thea and stroked her hair. The conditioner felt slippery and made her hair feel mushy. "I don't like this." He made a face. "How does it remove tangles?" He rubbed her hair between his fingers.

She continued to comb her fingers through her hair to remove the worst of the knots, edging a bit away from him. "It relaxes the hair and makes it slick so it can slide loose. It also keeps the strands from breaking as badly. I need to trim it too. I'm getting split ends." Ducking under the water again she combed the strands to help rinse the conditioner out. When she came up again Daeshen was reading the bottle with a frown of concentration. She held out the shampoo to Kyrin. "Would you like to try it?"

Her eyes widened as he stood and waded to them. *Damn, he's big!* He turned and presented his back to her.

"Would you do it?" he asked.

"O-okay." She quickly worked some of the sweet scented stuff into his hair. She bit her lip as his hair curled around her hands like an affectionate cat. She massaged his scalp with the pads of her fingers. A deep, husky hum of pleasure made her jump. He tilted his head back and sighed happily.

Kyrin looked up into her wide eyes and grinned. "I could get used to this." His grin widened when she blushed and quickly averted her eyes. He pulled away and rinsed the soap from his hair.

Daeshen set the bottle down and levered himself out of the tub. He grabbed a towel and quickly dried himself. Nude, he crouched in front of the cabinet again and started digging around. Taking out more bottles he started reading them. The others followed him out of the tub.

Kyrin snagged a comb from a drawer and stood behind Thea. Catching her heavy fall of hair he gently smoothed the tangles out. He had heard another male say that his mate found this very soothing and asked him to do it frequently. She stood very still and held the towel wrapped around her like a shield, but didn't pull away. After he finished he put on his robe and offered her one.

He grinned when Thea took it and quickly wrapped herself in the heated folds. She shifted from foot to foot nervously. Kyrin winked at her reassuringly.

"Come on, Dae, you can explore Theadora's things after breakfast." He quirked an eyebrow as Daeshen absently put on a robe without looking up from the bottle he was inspecting. Plucking the bottle from the other's hand, he ignored the grumbling and herded them through the door.

Chapter Five

Over a breakfast of bread, fruit and coffee both men told Thea a bit about themselves. Kyrin, she learned, was captain of the ship they were on, while Daeshen worked in the science department.

"We are primarily a science vessel." Kyrin took a cautious sip of the Terren coffee he had requested. He wrinkled his nose at the bitter, oily flavor. He set it down quickly, wondering why humans were so fond of it. "Our job is to collect samples from different planets and catalog them. We also look for other races with similar technology. If a race has achieved space travel we approach them and begin the initial diplomatic relations. If the race is interested in trade we send our findings back to our home planet where the rest of the negotiations are handled by our government. Trade is handled very carefully to avoid possible damage to both planets ecosystems."

Thea nodded, listening intently. She swallowed the bite of bread in her mouth and picked up her mug and took a sip. Her stomach heaved. Biting back the urge to spit it out she quickly swallowed. Setting the cup down, she shuddered. Whoever had brewed it had used enough coffee to choke a horse. The stuff was strong enough to melt steel. "Uh... Do you always drink coffee this strong?" Her tongue felt like it was going to crawl down her throat and hide. The memory of a cartoon flashed through her head. The character had stirred some sugar into their coffee and the end of the spoon had dissolved when it came out of the cup.

The men gazed down at the offending beverage. "It's not supposed to taste like that?" they chorused.

She shuddered again. "No."

Daeshen frowned. "Oh. We had it brought for you. Personally, I thought it was disgusting." He licked his lips and took another bite of fruit, trying to get the last of the taste out of his mouth. Like Kyrin, he had only drunk one or two sips of the foul brew.

Thea picked up the pot and stalked to the small sink and counter that lined one wall of the tiny kitchen area just off the small dining area. The men watched her turn on the hot water and pour out half of the coffee in the pot. She added more hot water to the pot. In an attempt to dilute the acidic stuff.

Mournfully, they watched her stalk back to the table, gather up all three cups and dump them in the sink as well. "*Is she going to make us drink more?*" Daeshen whined plaintively in Kyrin's head.

"*I think so,*" he sent back glumly, slumping in his seat.

They watched her sit down again. She poured herself another cup and sipped. "Well, that's better, but it's still not great. Do you have any cream and sugar?"

Daeshen sent a com requesting some, wondering how much of the foul stuff he was going to have to drink to make her happy. "It should be here soon," he mumbled.

Kyrin cleared his throat and began telling Thea about their duties aboard the ship. The door chimed softly a few minutes later. "Come in." A crewman entered, carrying a small platter with the requested items. He quickly set them down and exited without a word.

They watched Thea pour them each a cup of coffee; she then added cream and sugar to all three. She tasted hers, nodded and passed them the cups again. "At least it's drinkable now. Someone needs to have a talk with your cook."

They shot Thea a look.

She stared back expectantly.

Suppressing a sigh, Kyrin picked up his cup and waited for Daeshen to follow suit. Grimacing, he took a sip, expecting his mouth to be assaulted a second time. Much to his surprise, it wasn't nearly as bad. Judging by the look on Daeshen's face, he agreed.

Satisfied, Thea went back to eating her breakfast.

"*Why do I think we just passed a test we didn't know we were taking?*" Kyrin sent to Daeshen.

"*Probably because we were,*" Daeshen grumbled back.

"So, Theadora, what do you do? Somehow I don't think waiting tables was your chosen occupation," Daeshen asked her. He pushed the cup away from him with studied casualness.

She hurriedly swallowed the fruit in her mouth. "Oh, um, I weave fabric for a couple of designers who make period costumes. I also make tapestries. I sell them in booths at science fiction and fantasy conventions." She toyed with her food nervously. When they didn't laugh she looked up. They both looked interested, so she continued. "Some members of the SCA, that's the Society for Creative Anachronism, pay well for costumes made from hand woven and dyed fabric. Not very many people know how to do it anymore, so I've created a pretty good market for myself."

"My grandmother taught me before she died. She said that there was always a woman in our family that learned weaving in every generation." She stole another look from them. "I'm the last of our line, though. So, if I have children, I'll have to teach them. I was hoping to save enough money someday to buy some property. I wanted to try to raise animals and plants to make my own thread and wool." She stuttered to a stop. Now her dream would never happen. She blinked back tears. "I can never go home, can I?"

Kyrin sighed and leaned back in his chair. "Your home is with us now, love."

She nodded, staring down at the remains of her breakfast. She pushed the plate away as her appetite dwindled. A wave of misery washed over her. They had taken everything from her and she wasn't sure she wanted what they were offering as compensation. She had always hoped to find a nice man and settle down to raise a child or two. A partnership. Not being told how she was going to live her life and that she had no say in the decisions made concerning her. What she didn't understand was why she felt that she wanted them to comfort her when they were the ones that had caused her distress in the first place. *Guess Dad was always right; women don't make sense.*

Daeshen reached out and caught her chin; he lifted her eyes to meet his. "Just because you're with us now doesn't mean you can't still have your dream, love." He stroked her cheek with his thumb. "Weaving is a highly respected skill in our culture. I know there are several artisans on this ship who would be thrilled to work with you. And I don't see why you can't tell us what you need to make your own products. We have a large science lab. Just tell us what you need."

Kyrin nodded. "The plants can easily be grown in the hydroponics lab. If you tell us what animals you want, we can add them to our collection list. We've already collected several species. Anything we can't grow can be duplicated in the cloning units, as well. We just need samples."

Thea sniffled. She looked up at both of them. "You'd do that for me?" she asked in a small voice.

Daeshen pulled her into his lap and hugged her tight. "Of course. We want you to be happy; just give us a chance." He smiled when she cuddled closer to him and nodded. His hands stroked up and down her back in a comforting manner.

"And on that note, I need to get dressed for duties. Daeshen will be working here so you won't be alone." Kyrin stood and disappeared into a small room to dress.

Daeshen lifted Thea off his lap and stood. He tugged her up beside him and led her to a door. "Let's show you where everything is. We've added rooms to expand our quarters. A singles cabin was fine for just the two of us, but we felt it would be cramped for three. Since we will be spending quite a bit of time on the ship we also wanted to give you room for your work." The door slid open with a soft whoosh of displaced air. "After we finish our job here we will be taking our passengers home to Ta'e. Once that is done we will be given a new assignment. As our mate you'll be traveling with us."

Thea peeked into the small room. "Oh, pretty." Deep aqua green carpet covered the floor. The walls were painted a soft gray with delicate scrollwork the same shade as the carpeting. Throw pillows a few shades lighter green were strewn over a sunken area in the center of the room. "The couch was built into the floor?" She stepped down into the bowl shaped area. Her feet sank a few inches. "Hey! This is cool! Is this gel?" She bounced a little before sitting down and relaxing.

Daeshen smiled indulgently. "Yes, it has a four inch layer of heated gel. I'm glad you like it." He stepped down next to her. There was a small table rising from the center; it had a small keypad embedded in it. He pressed a few buttons and a screen shimmered into view on the wall in front of them. "This is our private recreation area, for watching vids and playing games." A few more buttons were pressed and the screen disappeared again. "Come, love, there's more for you to see." Grasping her wrist he tugged her up with him and led her into another room.

She gasped softly. The walls were covered with floor to ceiling bookshelves. There were three overstuffed chairs arranged in the center of the room. Small tables had been set beside each chair. Walking to the nearest shelf she inspected the titles. "I had these in my collection." She smiled sadly at the loss of her paper friends. Hearing Daeshen clear his throat she turned to him.

"We brought your possessions aboard, love." He smiled sheepishly. "We wanted you to have your own things. Normally we would just add books to our computer database, but we thought you would prefer to keep yours. We didn't take your videos, though. Well, you can go through everything and see."

She smiled and impulsively hugged him. "Thank you." A warm feeling crept over her. They really were trying to make her feel at home, and smooth the transition as much as they could.

He was showing her the other rooms containing her things when Kyrin called that he was leaving. Excusing himself, Daeshen left Thea to prowl her new territory and went to his office to work on some files.

* * *

Thea spent the remainder of the morning sorting through the rooms she had been given. There was a small room that would be good for her work. It looked like it was set up similarly to the dining area in their main quarters. Taking out a small notebook she wrote down a list of things she would need for her weaving, sewing and dying. Absently she rubbed her arm across her cheek. Her face and abdomen had been alternately itching and tingling faintly for the last hour. *Wonder if I'm allergic to the salt oils.*

She dug out the box containing her looms and began setting them up.

Several hours passed before she suddenly realized her stomach was beginning to loudly protest her skipped lunch. Setting aside what she was doing she went in search of Daeshen.

While they ate she asked him, hesitantly, to explain why his people were taking human women. The men had glossed over that subject during breakfast and she wanted more information than their very brief comments.

He carefully explained the virus that had rendered so many of their women barren and how difficult it would be to keep their population strong with such a large decrease in genetic diversity. He went on to explain how the Ta'e'sha had searched for a race that would be compatible.

There was hope that some of the girls who had not gone through puberty would still be fertile, but as yet none had been found. That hope had not been given up, though. Their race took an average of twenty years to become fertile. The Ta'e'sha had several stages of puberty they went through before their reproductive organs were completely developed.

Thea blinked in surprise at this revelation. She couldn't imagine being considered a child until she was in her twenties. He was just as surprised to hear that humans went through puberty around the time they turned into teenagers.

He turned gray when she casually mentioned teen pregnancies.

After lunch she went back to her workroom to finish setting up a set of shelves that her grandfather had made for her grandmother long before she was born. They were a series of tilted bins forming shelves to hold skeins of yarn and folded weavings. A pole at the top allowed a cloth to be strung across the top to keep dust out of the items.

Her hand paused over the warm, smooth finish of the red cedar. She stroked it gently, leaning forward to inhale the scent of the wood. *I need to oil the wood again; it's getting dry.* Suddenly, tears blurred her vision. Her lungs tightened in her chest, cutting off her air as a wave of panic struck her like a fist. *Oh Goddess... Oh God... I can't do this!*

She would never visit the graves of her family again. Her children wouldn't be like her. She fell to her knees and grabbed a half finished quilt and wadded it up in her arms. Curling her body around the cloth she screamed and sobbed into it, letting loose the fear, pain and panic in her mind.

Minutes that seemed like hours passed as she finally let everything out, trying to be quiet so Daeshen wouldn't hear her. She didn't want him to drug her again; he had forgotten to give her another dose after lunch.

An hour passed and at last she lay still. She drew in shuddering breaths every few minutes as her body calmed. Hair clung to the side of her face in sweaty tendrils. Her eyes and face felt swollen and raw, like someone had rubbed them with wet sand paper. Her nose was swollen shut and dripping. She rubbed her arm across her cheek and stared blankly at the shelves, still clinging to the quilt.

A warm breeze caressed her cheek, leaving a tingle in its wake. Suddenly, she remembered something her mother had told her when she was a child and had come home crying because the other children had made fun of her for being different and pushed her into a mud puddle.

Her mother had held Thea in her lap and gently wiped her tears away with a damp cloth. "Thea, honey, remember this: you cannot control everything that happens to you. Bad things will happen and good things will happen. You need both to become a full person. The only thing you can control is how you react to them. Learn to accept them; fight if you must, but choose your battles carefully. Accept the good gracefully with an open heart and share it if you can." Her mother's fingers tilted her chin up and she kissed young Thea's nose. "And always remember that a smile is a free gift that costs you nothing and can completely change a person's day." A plate of cookies and milk had followed the conversation, as they had most discussions of that nature through her whole childhood.

She wiped the tears from her face again and lay still, contemplating the memory. Her swollen eyes drifted closed while she thought, cuddling the quilt closer to her. *My family will always be with me. And my life will be what I make of it. I have to decide if it will be a bitter draft or a sweet wine.* She sighed deeply.

Chapter Six

One week later...

Kyrin frowned as he received notification that another woman had been put into stasis. She was showing the same symptoms that the other two women had begun to exhibit. Her mate had found her in the bathing facilities scraping the skin from her arms and legs with a knife and crying uncontrollably. He immediately took her to the medical area. When a technician approached her she started screaming and fighting like a wild thing. It had taken two men to hold her down while a third administered a sedative.

He sent the Chief Medic a com to have him come to his quarters after his shift ended to discuss the matter and review his findings. Kyrin was very disturbed by the lack of progress helping the women, as well as the medical team's inability to discover what was causing the problem. He made a few notes to have his security team interview the women's mates. *Hmmm. It might also be useful to see if we can track their movements aboard the ship. Maybe we can find a pattern.*

* * *

Kyrin groaned softly as he entered his quarters. He was covered in sweat and muttering curses as he rotated his shoulder. Wincing, he wandered into the bathing room and started running a bath. He had fallen awkwardly in the gym and pulled a muscle in his shoulder while trying to catch himself.

Digging through the bottles on a shelf, he located the therapy salts and poured a generous handful into the steaming water. Quickly stripping and sinking into the water he let out a heartfelt groan of relief. Softly mumbling the meditation chant he let his tail form in the water and swished it gently back and forth as his body relaxed and the salts eased the soreness in his muscles.

"Hey, love, the CM is coming tonight to discuss a matter with me. I've invited him to have his evening meal with us as well. I think it would be good for Theadora to meet him since he will be handling her medical care personally. Could you tell her we are having a guest and ask her to prepare a menu?" he sent to Daeshen.

"Of course." There was a brief pause. *"What's wrong?"*

"I fell in the gym and twisted my shoulder. I'm in the bath. I should be fine in a few minutes."

"Ahhh... I suppose if you're not feeling better by the time dinner is ready Corvin can take a look at you and make sure you didn't tear something again. He told you to be more careful last time."

Kyrin winced at the chiding note in Daeshen's voice. His mate had a way of making him feel like a small boy caught stealing sweet drops. Sinking lower in the water, he glowered. It did not help that he deserved it. Closing his eyes, he let his head sink under the water and breathed through the gills located just under his collarbones. The lightly salted water was a balm to his senses; it had been far too long since he had changed and swam for the pleasure of it. His gills felt a bit tender as the water passed through them, a sure sign he was not shifting often enough to keep them completely hydrated. Enjoying the peaceful moment he let himself drift in the water, and for the first time in several weeks he let his mind relax along with his body.

Sometime later the faint echo of footsteps reached him in the water. He stretched lazily thinking Daeshen had come in to wake him. Opening his eyes he met Thea's shocked, wide gaze. *Oops.* He sat up cautiously.

Thea's eyes ran up and down his body. The man she was just coming to accept as her mate was not really a man at all. She slipped into the water, completely fascinated, to get a better look. His tail was a dark amber-orange; each scale had a slightly darker rim of color edging it. The fins were huge translucent gold veils that waved slowly in the water. Her gaze made its way slowly back up his length. It dawned on her that his whole body was several shades of amber, each complementing the next perfectly. His skin was a dark golden-brown, like he spent a good portion of his time sunbathing. Now she realized that it was his natural skin color. Her eyes rested on his solemn face, taking in the hint of worry in his eyes, and the tense way he held his body.

She sat down hard in the water and reached out. Slowly sliding her fingers along his tail she looked up at him again. "You're a merman." She drew in a deep breath, still unable to believe what her senses were telling her. This was impossible. The merfolk were myth, they did not actually exist.

"No, I am Ta'e'shian. Some of us do bear a striking resemblance to your mythology, though." He watched her caress his tail gently and blew out a relieved breath. Maybe she wasn't going to go berserk on him after all. Then, he recalled her fascination with water myths. *It might be a good idea to add this information to the sublims, though. I'll have to ask the mated men how their mates reacted to finding out.*

"I always loved mermaids. I used to dream I was one." She spoke softly. "When I could afford to buy my own home I wanted to live near the ocean. It called to me." She leaned closer and slid both of her hands along his skin and scales. "Will our children be like you?"

Kyrin shifted a bit; he was growing aroused by her caresses. "Yes, we believe our genes will be dominant. Occasionally, there might be children born without the ability to *saras*, shift form, but it will be rare."

She looked up with tears in her eyes. "Thank you, this is like a dream for me." Thea leaned forward and pressed a shy kiss against his lips. Leaning back she gently ran her hands along his chest. "Do you have gills?"

She opened her mouth to ask more questions, but he stopped her by placing a finger over her lips. "I'll answer all of your questions later, love, but now we should get dressed for dinner." He checked the time on his cereb. "Our guest will be here soon."

Thea looked down and blushed faintly, just noticing that her wet blouse was making it clear she hadn't bothered with a bra today.

Kyrin ran his thumb along her cheekbones. She winced as his gentle touch stung the raw patches the rash had left on her skin. "What's this?"

"Oh." Thea pulled back a bit. "I think I'm allergic to the oils Daeshen puts in the bath. My face and stomach have been itching and burning all week. It's driving me crazy. My legs started feeling itchy a little while ago, too."

"Hmmm, the man who will be joining us for dinner is the ship's Chief Medic, his name is Corvin. I'll ask him to look at these spots; he's going to be handling your medical care." He smiled and kissed her gently. "What were you planning to serve for dinner?"

Thea sloshed her way out of the tub and stood, dripping on the rim. "Well, I was thinking about roast beef, roasted carrots and potatoes and warm French bread. But, the kitchen is so small and I don't know how to work the appliances, let alone where to get the ingredients. When is he supposed to join us?" She tried to wring the hem of her skirt. It didn't help. Sighing, she stripped and reached for a towel. She was absently aware of how quickly she was becoming accustomed to being nude in their presence. And lately she was aware of occasional flashes of knowledge that she should not have. She made a mental note to ask Kyrin about it later.

Kyrin watched appreciatively, then frowned when he saw the rash on her legs and stomach. "I'll show you how to use the kitchen, love." He changed his tail back to legs and strode from the water. Catching the edges of Thea's towel, he pulled her against him for a slow, leisurely kiss. "Corvin will be joining us in about two hours."

"Two hours? That's not enough to time properly prepare a roast!" she muttered.

He picked up her wet clothes and tossed them into a cleaning unit. He listened to Thea absently as he cleaned the bathing room and put away a few bottles of salt oil that had been left out. Bending down to wipe away some trailed water on the floor he was absently aware of his little mate quieting. He looked back and grinned as she guiltily met his eyes. "Like what you see?"

He laughed and tugged her against him for a quick kiss as her cheeks turned pink and she glowered at him. It was such fun to tease her.

* * *

Corvin inhaled appreciatively as soon as he stepped into the cabin. "What is that aroma?"

Daeshen grinned at him. "It seems Thea can cook. She's making something called 'pizza' and claims it's a staple food in her country. Kyrin showed her the kitchen and how everything works and she got a positively predatory look on her face. Then she kicked us out. Every once in awhile one of us checks on her and it looks like a windstorm went through a grocery store. I asked if she needed any help and she growled at me, muttered something about 'ice cream' and asked if we ate fungus. I left. Kyrin can check on her now."

Corvin laughed heartily at the look of repugnance on Daeshen's face. "Well, you should expect things like this, my friend. She's not Ta'e'shian; she is going to eat things that seem odd and even disgusting to us. I imagine we'll seem the same to her upon occasion. How is she dealing with the two of you?"

"We decided to give her small doses of a sedative the first few days, but she's doing really well. It helps that she has a very flexible personality. Kyrin had a brief period of worrying about hysterics when she walked into the bathing room tonight and he was relaxing. She saw his tail. But, she loves the water myths from her world and was excited instead." Daeshen led him into the dining area.

Corvin looked at the set table and smiled. He had often joined both men for meals, but they rarely cooked, usually ordering meals from the communal galley. It was nice to see that Thea was already making changes and creating a feeling of home in the cabin.

Kyrin darted out of the kitchen. "She has a temper. And don't ask what kind of meat is in the food. The description she gave me sounded horrifying." There was a shouted "I heard that!" from the kitchen. Kyrin grinned. "We probably should have started eating human foods before now, though."

Thea bustled out of the kitchen with a bowl of salad. She stopped and eyed Corvin with cool curiosity. "Hello."

He bowed briefly. "Nice to meet you, Theadora. My name is Corvin Sa'ama."

She set the bowl on the table and offered her hand. "Nice to meet you as well."

He shook it gravely. He was more familiar with human customs since he had had more contact with the women brought onboard.

"Well, dinner is ready. I didn't know what beverages you would like so I asked the galley to send cola and beer." She walked back into the kitchen, returning with two pitchers. One was filled with a black carbonated liquid, while the other held a foamy golden beverage. She set them on the table and motioned for the men to sit before returning to the kitchen.

Corvin quickly took a seat; he had found that he quite enjoyed most of the foods that had been introduced by the women brought aboard, and was eager to try another dish. Daeshen and Kyrin joined him, not looking nearly as enthusiastic. "Is something wrong?"

"We're hoping dinner isn't like coffee," Kyrin muttered. "She makes us drink it every morning and it's horrible."

"Hmmm, I don't think that will be the case. Coffee seems to be something of an art to make. And the galley crew hasn't mastered it yet. Haven't you noticed that most of the humans mix things in it or don't drink it? I've found that most of the women are making it in their quarters instead of drinking the stuff the galley serves." Corvin laughed softly at the arrested look on both men's faces.

Thea came out of the kitchen balancing a large round pan on a cloth. She carefully set it down in the center of the table and then took her seat between Kyrin and Daeshen. They looked down at her offering. A verity of sliced meats peeked out of artfully arranged vegetables. Melted cheese bubbled and steamed where it had been sprinkled over the top. She reached in and took the edge of the pizza and lifted a wedge of it onto her plate, then caught up the gooey strings of cheese that followed the slice. The men followed her example.

The meal continued, quietly punctuated by soft conversation and compliments. Both Kyrin and Daeshen were pleasantly surprised with the food and vocal in their appreciation of Thea's skills. Kyrin enjoyed the tart flavor of the cola beverage, but found the beer was too pungent for his taste

After they finished eating Thea cleared the table and brought out *valasa*, a Ta'e'shian tea that Daeshen liked to drink at lunch. She had tasted it and enjoyed the flavor and decided to serve that instead of coffee. Thea smirked to herself remembering the looks on her husbands' faces when she made them drink the coffee served by the galley. She made a mental note to see about acquiring a coffee pot since she could not find hers among her possessions. She slipped out after serving the men to finish putting her last loom together. She had moved the largest of her looms into the library as she had quickly run out of room in her workroom.

Corvin rubbed his full belly and leaned back in his chair. "You were right, Kyrin, the psychscans missed a few people. I'm having them speak with the *asana* regarding their fears of the human women joining us. Luckily it's only a few people. I sent a request to the other ships to check as well. I also sent a long range com back to Ta'e to notify them that the scans are missing people."

The conversation turned to the plight to the women in stasis after that. Corvin had attempted several sublim sequences that had not seemed to make any impression on the women. Since the asana, priests and priestesses, of the Balance Temple were unable to help, as the women were not telepathic, he was at a loss. Usually the mind healers in the Temple would be able to discover the cause immediately and begin treatment.

Thea returned as Corvin was beginning to describe the behavior of the women, before they were put into stasis, and how they acted when they were removed from it. A chill curled through her as she listened to the description of them crying, screaming and hurting themselves. Some simply lay on beds with blank eyes and keened softly to themselves. At least, until someone approached them, then they became screaming, fighting wild things. She pressed herself close to Kyrin. "It sounds like they were raped," she muttered softly.

Kyrin stiffened and looked up at her. "What did you say, love?"

She gulped when all three men stared at her. "Um, I said it sounds like they were raped."

Daeshen leaned back in his chair and blew out a breath. "Rape. We never even considered that. But how can we find out if the women can't be taken from stasis long enough to question them?"

Kyrin pulled his little mate into his lap, shaken by the thought. Ta'e'shian women were as strong as their men; as a result rape was very uncommon in their society. That combined with the mind healers and truth sayers of the Balance Temple making it so difficult for the offender, or offenders, to remain undetected it had become a virtually unknown crime. "Human women are smaller than we are and not as strong," he mused aloud.

Corvin tapped a finger on the table. "How can we interview them, though? We need to discover if that's what happened. Now that Thea has brought it up, their symptoms are very similar. But one of the women had seizures when we tried to bring her out. I'm at a loss."

Thea tucked her head under Kyrin's chin. "What are you doing? Are men present when they are woken up? Have you asked a therapist to see them? Did you take any samples before you placed them in stasis?"

Corvin pulled a holoreader out of his pocket and made some notes. "No, we haven't done any of that, but we will. We don't have therapists, as you know them, though."

She shrugged. "Well, you have how many human women here? See if there are any psychologists, psychiatrists or rape counselors among them."

The men blinked. Kyrin cleared his throat. "Ahhh, well, we haven't collected any information about their careers." He winced when her head shot up, clipping him on the chin.

Thea's eyes narrowed as she glared at him. "Well then, you better get your ass in gear, Captain. We have skills to offer and if you think we're just gonna be broodmares for you, you had better think again." She got up and stomped into the bedroom.

Corvin cleared his throat. "She brings up a good point. We need to integrate the woman into our society. I'll ask the asana to begin interviewing them and help find places for them in their fields. Daeshen, please bring Thea to the medical area tomorrow so I can take some samples. I'll see what I can find out about that rash." He made a few more notes on his holoreader before thanking them for dinner and taking his leave.

Daeshen and Kyrin looked at each other, then turned and looked at the door Thea had gone through.

Daeshen cleared his throat. "You go first." He grabbed the cups off the table and scampered into the kitchen before Kyrin could reply.

"Coward," he muttered.

* * *

Thea grumbled under her breath about brainless, arrogant men as she dug through her clothes for a nightgown. Finding several items she had decorated their bedroom with she started displaying them around the room while she contemplated tying Kyrin up and beating his ass this time. Finishing, she stepped back and nodded, pleased with the look of the room. It was a bit homier now. Snatching up her nightgown she strolled toward the bathing area for a shower. She shot Kyrin a peeved look from the corner of her eye as she sailed past him.

Kyrin snagged her waist before she made it out of the room. He snuggled her stiff little body against his and kissed her throat. "You have to have some patience, love. We're new at this, too." He trailed kisses along her cheeks.

"Hrumph, we'll see." She looked up at him with sad eyes. "Your people need to accept us, or we'll never accept you." She slipped free of his arms and went into the bathing area.

The faint sound of the door shutting seemed to echo loudly in Kyrin's ears. He knew she was right and he was doing everything he could to try and integrate the women to his ship and people. A faint smile stretched his lips as a thought hit him. *Maybe I should ask for some help and advice...* He left the bedroom for the office and settled in at his computer desk. He quickly sent several requests out before logging back out and heading back to the bedroom, now humming happily under his breath. The sight of Daeshen removing his clothes brought him to a stop.

Daeshen looked over his shoulder as he heard Kyrin come in. He winked slowly and let his uniform fall to a pool around his feet. Stepping free of the clothing he slid boneless onto the bed and watched his mate with half-closed eyes.

Rolling onto his back he scooted to the edge of the bed. "Come here…" His voice was a sultry growl.

Kyrin smiled and strolled slowly to the bed, admiring Daeshen's pale skin against the deep purple sheets. "Is there something you want, my love?" He ran a finger along Daeshen's shoulder.

Daeshen smiled, reaching out to release the closures on Kyrin's uniform. "Yes, I believe there is…" Reaching inside Kyrin's clothing he caressed the hard planes of his stomach.

* * *

Thea stood under the hot spray of water. Showers were something she had always found relaxing, and felt they cleansed more than just her body. Tilting her face into the spray she spoke softly, talking to the only beings left to her to find comfort and answers from. "Lord and Lady, bless me for I am your child. I am torn and conflicted and would request your wisdom." She took a deep breath and slowly let it out, repeating the action several times to clear her mind and form her thoughts before speaking them aloud. Once she felt calm sweeping over her she began to speak.

She quietly outlined the events of the last few days, and her attraction to the two men who had claimed her. Her head tilted down, the hot water washed down her back in comforting streams. Thea's family had practiced the old ways for generations. They had quietly gone about their lives, moving when the neighbors began to ask too many questions. It was a habit they hadn't broken even after their religion had become more accepted; it was too ingrained in them. As a result they had fewer ties than most people, and relied on each other more. The deaths of her family members had hit her hard, leaving her alone in more ways than simply missing their presence. It had shaken her faith and left her a solitary practitioner.

She quietly finished her recital and ended it with her questions. "Do I give them my trust? Should I take these men as my husbands? Will this new path lead me where I am supposed to go?" Sometimes a response was forthcoming, at other times she felt nothing. Turning to the steamy walls she traced out the word yes and the word no. Placing a hand under each word, she waited.

Minutes passed. Just as she was about to give up the hand under the word yes pulsed with gentle heat three times. The feeling of warm arms surrounded her in a brief hug. She drew in a deep breath. "Thank you, Lord and Lady, I love you, too. I give you the energy of fear and uncertainty. I no longer need them, please use this energy in a more positive manner than I have thus far." The heavy weight that had been lurking over her heart lifted and she stepped out of the shower to dry herself. She felt that she had reaffirmed her decisions and choices to accept these changes in her life and make the best of them.

Tossing her nightgown into the laundry chute she squared her shoulders. Holding her head high she strode into the bedroom nude. The sight that met her eyes made her come to a full stop. *Whoa.*

Her husbands had apparently decided not to wait for her. As she watched Daeshen rolled onto his back and stroked his tongue slowly from the base of Kyrin's cock to the crown where he paused for a moment to tickle the frills gently. Her eyes widened; she had never seen anything like this before. Heat pooled in her belly. *Wow, this is better than my stories!* Both men had their eyes closed as Daeshen sucked the strong column into his mouth and stroked his palm along the remaining length.

Thea padded closer on silent feet. She watched Kyrin's face as his breath became harsher. Daeshen hummed softly and raised his head to take more of Kyrin's cock into his mouth; a soft suckling sound broke the silence as his mouth moved rhythmically. She crept around the edge of the bed. Holding her hair back she leaned down and swirled her tongue along the weeping tip on Daeshen's cock. He jumped and mumbled something around Kyrin's cock as his eyes shot open. He looked down at her in surprise.

Thea smiled and crawled onto the bed. She leaned down and took him into her mouth again. Daeshen moaned deep in his throat and arched up to meet her. It was the first chance she'd had to explore their bodies and she intended to take full advantage of it. Curling her tongue she lapped the fluid leaking from the tip of his glans; it was sweet and had a faint licorice flavor. It was not at all what she had expected it to taste like. She slowly explored the frills that spiraled around it. They trembled against her tongue. Licking her way down, she opened her eyes and glanced up to where Daeshen was lazily stroking Kyrin's cock in and out of his mouth. Her gaze traveled up Kyrin's strong form; he was watching both of them with heavy lidded eyes.

She inspected him closely; the head of his cock was flushed a dark purple while the frills were the same color as his hair. Her tongue curled under his frills and tickled gently. Each of the frills had hundreds of tiny flexible spines imbedded in it. It was an odd sensation to have them fluttering anxiously against her lips and tongue.

Daeshen groaned harshly and arched into her touch. Lifting her head she stroked her hand gently up and down his shaft. She pursed her lips, watching the men move together in a familiar rhythm. Thea's hands smoothed over Daeshen's hips, tracing the delicate bones under his skin. Her tongue swirled wet patterns over his balls, pausing for a moment to tickle the small hairs curling around them. Daeshen shuddered in response. Deciding to stop teasing him she lifted her mouth away from him, lazily stroking his cock with firm pressure.

Straddling Daeshen's body she slinked up to trace her tongue along his lips where they were wrapped around Kyrin's shaft. Licking her way up Kyrin's belly she stopped at his throat and nibbled on it experimentally for a moment. He tasted musky and warm. She licked her lips, deciding she liked his taste. Pressing her body close to his she pulled his head down to hers. Nibbling lightly along his lips she neatly eluded his attempts to deepen the kiss. She wanted to explore more before they took over. And she knew they would.

Kyrin growled softly. He cupped her ass and pulled her teasing body closer to his. She felt so good pressed against him. Daeshen's mouth moved hot and wet around his cock. Occasionally his teeth scraped over the sensitive skin. Kyrin shuddered with apprehension, slowly kneading the plump ass in his hands as he let her play.

Kyrin listened as Daeshen murmured his appreciation of the view being presented to him. He moaned as the other man released his cock and began to gently mouth his balls, licking and suckling on the soft skin gently but firmly. He

to escape. Small helpless screams echoed in the chamber as he continued his measured application of pain. Finally, he stopped and massaged the dark pink skin with firm hard strokes while she lay still under him, panting. He pressed her ass apart again, admiring the glistening shine of oil coating the virgin territory.

He watched as Daeshen gently pressed the tip of the oiled plug against it and began to press it slowly in. Her virgin ass mushroomed around the thick plug. As Kyrin watched the plug work its way into her he rubbed her skin soothingly and murmured soft reassurances.

Thea's eyes bulged as she felt something much thicker than a finger slowly begin to force itself into her abused ass. She moaned in pain; it felt as if it were tearing her in half. Swaying her hips in distress, she tried to fight the urge to pull away, she did not want Kyrin to spank her and she knew that if she did pull away it would start all over again. The object continued to tunnel into her for what seemed like hours, until finally she felt Daeshen's fingers brush against her hot skin. His fingers began to massage gently around the swollen and tightly spread skin surrounding whatever he had forced into her. Suddenly she felt the object begin to swell and contract inside her and Daeshen's hands left her.

Kyrin and Daeshen released her and slid away from her body. Thea fell onto her hip and trembled. "Oh Goddess…" The plug inside her started to stretch deeper and then pull back slowly while it swelled and contracted. "What did you put in me?" She shuddered. The men grasped her shoulders and legs, and twisted her around to the front of the bed before turning her onto her back. Daeshen pulled her up into a sitting position, forcing a soft scream from her as the plug shifted with the movement. Kyrin set some pillows behind her and Daeshen pressed her back into them, making her moan as the plug was shifted again and continued it devilish motions.

They drew her hands above her head and tied them. Next they looped cords around her knees and pulled them up and to the side, forcing her legs up and apart, then tying them off as well. Thea shuddered, as her thoughts became a hazy blur of embarrassment and desire. She lay there completely exposed to their eyes while the plug worked her ass, stretching and opening her for their later pleasure.

Kyrin hummed softly and kissed Daeshen's throat. "Lovely, we should do this often. I can't wait to get into her ass." Daeshen moaned softly at his words and pressed closer. They caressed each other as they watched Thea writhe against her bonds while the device inside her pulsed and thrust. Kyrin curled his fingers around Daeshen's neck and bent him forward, toward Thea's exposed clit, with gentle pressure.

Daeshen purred softly with pleasure, lapping slowly from her seeping channel up to where her hard little clit was peeking out from its hood. Winding his arms around her thighs to hold her still he thrust his tongue hard and deep inside her to lick at her inner walls and sup upon her juices. He felt Kyrin press oiled fingers into his ass and moaned in anticipation.

The other man's fingers rasped against the tight ring as they forged their way in. They withdrew briefly before returning and twisting smoothly to spread the oil deeper. Kyrin's hands tugged at his shoulder. He sat up and Kyrin's hand grasped his cock and guided it to Thea's weeping slit and teased it slowly up and down and in small circles around her clit, drawing soft groans from both of them. Centering it against the wet opening of her body he urged Daeshen inside with a firm hand on his hip.

Daeshen moaned at the tight wet grip of Thea's pussy. He felt the plug moving inside her just on the other side of a thin barrier of skin. Reaching out he caught her breasts in his hands and stroked them slowly, like he was petting something small, soft and divine to the touch. He settled his knees under her upraised, tied thighs.

His eyes locked with Thea's as he pushed his way inside her. The plug and the position of her body pressed him hard into her. At last he came to rest against her, her tight pussy gripping him like a glove. The hair at the base of his cock twisted through the rings piercing her lips, holding her open and tight against him. They writhed gently around her clit. He pressed harder against her when she bucked under him. He could feel the plug moving inside her. It throbbed against his cock with each of its delving motions.

Daeshen felt Kyrin's hands part his ass. The crown of the other man's glans nudged him before it began to press gradually into the dark heat of his body. Kyrin's hands grasped his hips firmly as they began to sway leisurely in response to Thea's wet grasp and the slow penetration of his ass. Kyrin nuzzled Daeshen's hair away from the back of his neck and a soft lap caressed him before teeth bit down firmly on the sensitive nape of his neck. The other man's fingers tightened on his hips as, with a grunt, Kyrin seated himself fully. His eyes closed as Kyrin began to thrust languidly within him.

All three of them groaned at the sensation.

Daeshen's hands squeezed Thea's breasts in time to each measured intrusion and withdrawal. He held himself tight to her, letting Kyrin's movements grind his abdomen against her clit. His deeper cries twined and sailed in the air with her softer ones. He rested he forehead against hers. The sensation of penetrating and being penetrated pushed him closer to the edge. Closing his eyes tightly he fought his impending climax, this moment was far too delicious to end so quickly. He felt echoes of Kyrin's pleasure along their mental link and shared the sensations coursing through his body with him.

Thea panted softly and tilted her head back to catch Daeshen's mouth, twining her tongue around his. Her body clenched voraciously around his heavy fullness. His heavy grinding and rasping hair slid hotly along her burning nub. He growled softly into her mouth. He bucked his hips against her, making her cry out as another inch eased in. Lifting his head, he smiled at the way her hands clenched and pulled against the bindings wrapped around her wrists.

Daeshen's head dropped onto her shoulder as he began to make small thrusts in and out of her wet flesh, aided by Kyrin's forceful movements inside him.

"Oh Goddess..." Daeshen moaned softly, he leaned back and rested against Kyrin's chest and shuddered. "Coming..." His hands squeezed her breasts spasmodically as his dick jerked and shot hot streams of cum into her. The strands rasping her clit picked up speed, forcing her to come with him, tearing a scream from her throat.

She thrashed against her bonds as shivers racked her body. "Oh yes!" She found the feeling of him ejaculating inside her unbearably exciting. His frills stroked and fluttered inside her, driving another small orgasm and weak buck of her hips. Her body drank deeply of him, taking each hot jet into her womb.

Kyrin smiled in a pained fashion as he listened to Thea's crooning encouragement. Her eyes opened and caught his over Daeshen's shaking shoulder. Shifting the position of his knees, his thrusts picked up speed. Never taking his eyes from hers he rolled his hips in a voluptuous movement and was rewarded by Daeshen picking up the pace of his small thrusts

Kyrin laughed hoarsely, continuing to work his prick in and out of Daeshen. Every few thrusts another small orgasm made Thea cry out softly. He felt his balls pull tight against his body and groaned as the tension burst in a blinding wet flash inside Daeshen. Panting softly Kyrin pressed small kisses along the back of Daeshen's neck and Thea's lips.

Thea bucked weakly; the plug was still moving inside of her. Its steady slow movements continued to drive her body to climax after climax. She murmured wordlessly into Kyrin's mouth. She felt his lips curve into a smile when she stiffened and cried out softly again.

Daeshen raised himself off Thea's shoulder after a few moments and smiled down at her. Kyrin rested his chin on Daeshen's shoulder and stroked his belly gently. He turned his head and pressed a gentle kiss onto Kyrin's cheek. "Precious ones." He reached up and released the cords binding her. Rubbing his hands over the balls of her shoulders he gently soothed any stiffness away. She curled her legs around both men after he released them.

Thea blushed and looked up at Kyrin shyly. "Can you take it out now? It's driving me crazy!" Her back arched as the waves of pleasure began to rise again. She whimpered softly. "Oh!"

Kyrin laughed softly and slowly disengaged himself from Daeshen's body. He tugged Daeshen out of Thea as well and unwound her legs from his waist.

Daeshen yawned and moved to lie on his side by Thea. Leaning over her he lapped gently at her nipples, making her groan.

Kyrin slid his hand along Thea's soaking slit and tapped the base of the plug to stop its movement before slowly pulling it free.

Thea cried out and contracted around it as it came loose. Stars burst behind her eyes as she trembled her way through yet another orgasm. Her mate laughed softly and pressed a gentle kiss to her lips before he stood and strolled lazily into the bathing room with the plug.

Daeshen curled himself around Thea and hummed softly into her ear. He rubbed her belly with slow gentle circles. He kissed her jaw softly, "I love you, dearest," he murmured softly.

She turned her head and smiled at him.

Kyrin padded back in and climbed into the bed and covered the three of them with a blanket. Leaning over he kissed them both and then curled his body tightly along Thea's other side.

Both men sighed contentedly and fell asleep almost immediately.

Thea stayed awake, thinking. Thoughts chased each other in her head, while she tried to decide what to do next. She was starting to feel like she had a family again. That thought caused a small curl of happiness to bloom in her heart. She savored the feeling. *Maybe things will be okay after all.*

Her eyes finally began to grow heavy about an hour later and just before she closed them to drift off to sleep they were drawn to where both men had their hands resting protectively over her womb. She smiled sleepily to herself and snuggled deeper into their embrace to sleep.

* * *

Cool eyes watched from across the recreation room as several of the newly mated human females talked quietly amongst themselves at a table. An eyebrow arched silently as an unmated man approached them and struck up a conversation. The watcher casually picked up the drink on the table and strolled to a window near the table. Settling in a chair close enough to listen, the watcher took out a holoreader and pretended to be engrossed in its contents.

The man at the table was asking the women how they liked living on the ship and their new lives. The women responded quietly, discussing the changes in their lives.

The watcher made a few notes on the reader, and looked up, memorizing the people at the table, male and female. The man seemed to being paying a bit more attention to a small, curvy redhead than to the other women. Casually finishing the drink and snapping the holoreader shut the watcher stood and left the room unnoticed.

Chapter Seven

Thea yawned and stretched lazily, then rolled onto her belly. The room was empty except for her. She absently scratched her hip and looked around blearily. "Coffee." Smacking her lips, she grimaced. "Toothbrush." Dropping her chin back onto the bed, she stared blankly at the wall while her brain struggled toward wakefulness.

One thought stood out in her head. She wanted coffee and she wanted it now. But, just thinking of yesterday's offering almost brought tears to her eyes. "I want a triple shot caramel latte!" she whined softly to herself. "I'm from the Pacific Northwest, damn it! How the hell am I supposed to survive without a coffee shop on every corner?" she pouted. Visions of biscotti and scones danced in her head.

She rolled herself off the bed and shuffled into the bathing area to brush her teeth, still whining under her breath. She was *not* a morning person. Digging through the shelf she had seen Daeshen take her shampoo from she quickly located her toothbrush and paste. Moments later she had a froth of foam in her mouth as she busily scrubbed off what felt like an entire fur coat from her teeth. Little twinges of pain reminded her of all the unfamiliar activity her body had been subjected to in the last few days. And, to add insult to injury, her butt itched.

Still scrubbing her teeth she turned and looked down the length of her body. She glowered. No decent coffee. Kinky sex maniacs. Funky body piercings. *And now she had some weird rash on her ass!* It was more than any woman should have to bear.

Bending, she spit out the toothpaste and rinsed her mouth. Looking at her reflection balefully she noticed two tattoos just off center of the base of her throat. *Great. Piercings AND tattoos. Maybe I should change my name to Candy and buy a freakin' Harley!* She snarled at her reflection and stomped back into the bedroom.

Daeshen stood in the center of the room holding a steaming mug and covered plate. "Good morning, darling!" He smiled brightly at her.

She growled at him. *Ech! A morning person.*

He blinked.

Her eyes focused on the mug with predatory interest. She sniffed the air like a cat scenting a particularly juicy mouse.

He extended the mug warily. "I got this for you. Shana said it's Colombian dark roast."

She snatched the mug from him with a muttered thank you and cradled it like the gift from the Goddess it was. Taking a cautious sip she almost moaned in pleasure. It was rich, full bodied and redolent with the taste of cream and sugar and just a dash of cinnamon. "Ohhh yesss..." She shivered, almost feeling the caffeine infusing her veins. Plopping down onto the bed she cradled the mug between both of her palms and ignored the bite of toothpaste mixing with the coffee and took another sip of heaven.

Daeshen cautiously sat down next to her. He had a look on his face that suggested he was a little surprised by her surly attitude this morning. By the time she had finished half of the coffee she no longer felt it was necessary to keep giving him evil little looks of warning. She eyed the plate he was offering to her.

"Umm, this is for you, too," he said, scooting a bit away from her when she took it.

Thea decided she was human after all, and maybe she would not kill Daeshen for being a morning person. Maybe. She took the plate and set her mug on the bedside table. Peeking under the cover she found a blueberry bagel with cream cheese. "Ooooh yeeeeaaaahhhh." Looking up at her husband she smiled with pleasure and kissed him softly. "Thank you."

Daeshen relaxed. "What is it?" He peered at the plate.

"It's a bagel," she said in a reverent tone of voice. "With cream cheese." She offered him a bite, apparently feeling generous with the bearer of coffee and breakfast.

Daeshen chewed thoughtfully. "Mmm, this is good." He watched his little mate munch with her eyes closed and a blissful expression. An idea formed in his mind and he made a mental note to speak with Kyrin about it this evening. He wrapped an arm around her when she cuddled against his side and offered him another bite of her bagel.

Thea looked at him from under her lashes and offered him a drink of her coffee. He sipped cautiously, not wanting to try it, but not wanting to offend her. He hummed in startled pleasure over the taste. It wasn't horrible!

"Good, huh?" she asked with a grin.

"Uh huh. Much better. Is this what it's supposed to taste like?"

"Yup." She recovered her cup and took another long swallow. "Oh, yeah, much better."

Her nose twitched. *Hmmm... Vanilla...* She nuzzled Daeshen's neck. It was him. *Nice!* She inhaled deeply, he smelled like vanilla and musk. *Yum! Not just for girls anymore!* She set down her now empty cup and curled her arms around his waist and nibbled on his neck.

He laughed softly and slipped free of her hold. "Time to get dressed, we have an appointment in medical in about thirty minutes."

Pouting, she heaved herself off the bed and into the other room to clothe herself.

* * *

Corvin neatly placed a small bandage over the area he had just drawn blood from. His assistant carried all the samples and implements away on a tray. "That should take care of it. I'll com you as soon as I get the results from the tests." He gave Thea a small packet. "This is a general antihistamine; if it is an allergy these should calm the symptoms down until we find out what's causing it. Take one each morning."

She nodded and tucked the packet into a pocket. "Thanks, Corvin." She hopped off the examination table. Looking up, she caught the intense, dispassionate gaze of Corvin's assistant. She smiled. Flustered, he looked back down at what he was doing, his dark green hair knotting up behind him in agitation. Her smile faded as she watched him.

He looked up again, locking gazes with her. Shadows passed across his eyes. Thea felt her own gaze chill slightly. Something about him wasn't right. The assistant looked away again and quickly left the room. She watched him with uneasy curiosity.

Daeshen caught her hand and drew her to his side. "Please join us for dinner tomorrow night, Corvin," he said warmly. "Thea says she has some more recipes she wants to try."

"I'd be delighted!" came the reply. "What are you two going to do today?"

"I'm going to introduce Thea to Shana, Whist's mate, then we are going to look for a coffee pot."

"Ahhh... Well, I believe they have several in the galley." He turned to Thea. "What did you have planned for dinner tomorrow night? I quite enjoyed the pizza."

She smiled shyly. "Roast and vegetables."

He grinned. "Delightful, I believe I had that in the galley not too long ago." He walked them out, still chatting about the different foods he had tried. They left a few minutes later after exchanging farewells.

Corvin returned to his office and left a list of the tests he wanted his assistant to run on the samples. That completed he contacted the asana, priests, attending the Balance Temple and asked them to begin interviewing the human women regarding their careers. Once that list was completed he asked them to send the report to the captain, along with a list of any volunteers who would like to assist in helping to place the women in positions.

* * *

Thea strode happily back into their quarters carrying her new coffee pot. She had enjoyed meeting Shana. The woman was intelligent and had a cutting sense of humor. With short sun-streaked brown hair, lively hazel eyes, and a slightly plump figure she had an appealing aura that drew people to her. She had just sold her bakery in Northern California before she had been brought aboard and had been planning to move to a small town on the Washington coast to open another. Suffice it to say that her plans had been changed for her and now she was drifting while she tried to decide what to do.

Daeshen had left the two of them alone while he went on his quest to find a coffee pot for Thea. It had been an interesting chat. She smiled wryly to herself thinking about Kyrin's claim that she was going to be kept isolated until she was pregnant.

Shana was worried that there was no place on the ship for a woman with her skills since the Ta'e'sha did not seem to focus on food the way so many humans did. While they enjoyed good food it was not an area they spent a lot of time expanding. Several of the other women felt the same way she did about their own skills and careers.

Thea set her pot on the kitchen counter. She trailed her fingers along the clean steel edge of the small sink. It seemed she was luckier than she had known. Kyrin and Daeshen had gone to a great deal of trouble to make her comfortable, although it seemed that the Ta'e'sha made every effort to bring as many of the possessions of the women they brought aboard as possible. But, really, that's all they were. Possessions.

She drifted through the rooms, toward her new workshop. Leaning against a wall she studied the looms. Scanning the room, she took in the drafting table, skeins of yarn peeking out of boxes and pads of graph paper.

Seating herself at the table she drew a pad of paper to her. Taking a pencil she began to work on a new design for a tapestry. She let her thoughts work their way out with each stroke of her pencil. Every curve and line eased the pressure building. No matter how hard she tried to accept everything it still overwhelmed her sometimes. *I guess I should expect that, though. It's not like there have been a few small changes...*

* * *

Daeshen sat on the corner of Kyrin's desk and finished outlining his idea. "So, if we make space next to the galley we could possibly set up a restaurant or two and a coffee shop. I think it would give several of the women a project and also a place they would be comfortable spending their time. I was also remembering several members of the science team saying that it would be nice to have a few more recreational places since we are spending longer periods of time traveling than we have in the past."

Kyrin smiled. "That's an excellent idea. As soon as the asana have completed the interviews we'll start implementing it. But for now we can start making space for the new areas. I'll see to it this afternoon."

Daeshen slid off the desk and stole a quick kiss before turning to leave. "Oh, by the way, Corvin said that Thea's name mark is ready. We can have them placed this evening, if you wish." He was referring to the tattoos the Ta'e'shians had placed around their throats to denote their married status and the name of their mate or mates.

Kyrin grinned and nodded. "Sounds good."

He returned the smile and left. He decided to stop and see how things were proceeding with his science team before he returned to his quarters. Humming softly to himself as he strode down the hall he absently decided on lunch and dinner menus and sent a com to the galley to have them delivered at the appropriate times.

* * *

Two hours later Thea stared down at the sketch she had made. It featured several nude women at the edge of a cliff. Some cowered in huddled balls while others crouched in defensive positions. A few screamed their defiance, backs arched and heads thrown back. And a single figure stood serenely at the very edge of the cliff, face upturned to the storm that raged around them all. Two other women knelt on either side of her, reaching toward something at the bottom of the cliff. Faces swirled through the dark clouds and peered down at them. Bare, grasping branches of dark trees seemed to reach for the women. At the base of the cliff several mermen reached toward the women beseechingly from the foamy, storm tossed waters, their eyes dark and sad.

She blew out a breath and nodded to herself. Turning to her loom, she started threading it in readiness for the new tapestry. She did not know what she would do with it, but she knew that she had to make it.

Chapter Eight

One week later...

Thea looked around curiously, not recognizing where she was. The vast area surrounding her was a black void; some buried instinct warned her that she could walk forever and not come to the end.

Strange little swirls of iridescent mist danced alongside her, just out of reach, casting off a pale wispy luminescence. The faint sound of singing drew her attention. Turning, she followed the sound. The air felt strange here, as if she were pushing her way through water.

As she drew closer she could begin to distinguish different voices in the song. Deep male voices added a rumbling bass that she felt vibrate along her spine, while silky female tones shivered along her nerve endings. Suddenly, several of the swirls danced madly around her; she stopped, gasping as the light disoriented her. Closing her eyes she reached out as vertigo struck, making her sway as her balance became uncertain. The song ended abruptly. A moment later a large warm hand grasped hers, holding her steady. Her eyes opened and she stared up at the imposing face several feet above her.

The man looked as if his face and form had been carved from the finest white marble. Heavy masses of thigh length, snowy white hair writhed along his body, which was covered in glowing white scales from his waist to the tip of his huge fantails. His skin had just a hint of color and was tattooed; at least she assumed they were tattoos, with soft, glowing white filigree. Pale gray eyes smiled down at her, his hand squeezed hers reassuringly for a moment before he released her. A woman who could have been his twin flowed up to them and curled her tail around his. The movement seemed completely unconscious, as if they could not be standing near each other without touching. The woman smiled down at Thea, reaching out to stroke her cheek gently.

"Hello, niece, we've been waiting for you," she said in a soft lyrical voice.

Thea gasped as the woman's voice washed over her, echoing along each muscle and bone. She felt like harp strings being absently plucked. It brought to mind all the tales of the power in a mermaid's voice. How a song could enchant a sailor to jump overboard, only to drown seeking to hear it again.

The woman smiled gently. "I am Byasuen, this is my mate, Ecoha. We would ask your permission to use your voice to address Our children." Behind her several more of the tall, ethereally beautiful people floated closer, forming a semi-circle around the white couple. There were four more couples, each a matched set in shades of red, gray, black and aquamarine.

With a start Thea finally recognized them. They were the Gods and Goddesses of the Ta'e'sha. Daeshen had started to tell her about them just the day before. "Umm, yeah, I guess so," she mumbled softly, feeling overwhelmed and wondering why they wanted her. And why they were calling her "niece."

"Thank you, niece, We will not take long. Nor will We hurt you in anyway, but best We hurry. Your mates are becoming concerned for you." Byasuen laughed softly. "My, they are protective, one would think they were Your sons, Kashka."

The black Goddess grinned wickedly. "As it should be, all mates should feel the warrior rise at a possible threat to their mate." She winked at Thea slowly with a pure black eye. "Especially when that mate carries life. And such beautiful life, but you'll understand soon, niece."

Kashka kissed Byasuen on the cheek. "You've chosen well, My Sister. She is giving and sweet. I agree with Your request; such an addition of gentleness could only benefit all Our children. So many of My children forget those qualities; I can only hope one notices and wishes to bask in her sunlight."

The men laughed, their deep voices rolling gently across her like distant thunder. The aquamarine one, Mo'aton, if Thea remembered correctly, spoke. "Oh, I think there is no doubt that some will wish to 'bask' in her." He winked at her playfully, making Thea blush profusely as she caught his meaning.

As one they began to hum softly, the sound oozing into her and making her dizzy. Gentle hands eased her to the ground as the world went dark.

* * *

Daeshen looked up from his holoreader and frowned as a soft sound came from the bedroom where Thea was taking a nap. He and Kyrin were worried. The rash on her legs, abdomen and face seemed to be even more swollen and raw this morning. Thea had awakened exhausted from her restless night. After working on a weaving project for a bit she had come to tell him she was going to take a nap and try to catch up on her sleep. Daeshen was hoping Corvin would contact them soon with some idea what the problem was. Hearing the sound again he stood and walked quickly into the bedroom.

His mate was writhing slowly under the light sheet she had pulled over herself before going to sleep. As he reached the bed her cheeks began to ooze tiny drops of blood where the skin had peeled and broken. Worriedly he looked down. The sheet had small, growing spots of crimson where more blood was beginning to cause it to cling wetly to her legs and stomach. Moaning softly with fear he sent a mental picture to Kyrin and ripped the sheet off of her. Tiny drops of blood continued to well up. He sent a com to the CM asking him to come to their quarters immediately. Taking her hands in his he called to her softly, trying to wake her up.

She did not respond other than to mutter under her breath in a language he did not recognize. It sounded like his own, but different. Suddenly her eyes flew open and she stared blankly up at the canopy of the bed for a moment before closing them again, now leaking tears of blood. Almost in tears himself he pulled her into his arms and cradled her nude form gently against him as Kyrin burst into the room.

Kyrin quickly assessed the situation. Daeshen had never handled dangerous or stressful situations well; he stopped thinking and only reacted. Checking his com to see how quickly the medics would be arriving, he slowly approached his mates. He carefully crawled onto the bed and checked Thea over, while Daeshen sang softly to her, trying to comfort them both.

A soft chime announced the entrance of the medics. Corvin bustled into the room, looking worried. "Computer, begin log: medical emergency, captain's quarters, input date and time. Visual and audio, please." Another medic followed behind him. A deep, threatening growl erupted from Daeshen's throat as they approached the bed, bringing both men to a quick stop. Not taking his eyes from the growling male Corvin spoke softly to Kyrin. "You need to bring him down so we can help her. I'd rather not have to sedate him, but his eyes are bleeding to hunting black, Kyrin."

He waited while Kyrin reached out to stroke Daeshen's neck gently to draw his attention. The amber haired man bent over Daeshen and spoke softly in his mate's ear, reassuring him that the men were going to help Thea, it was safe to let her go. Slowly the growling faded away.

Daeshen drew in a shuddering breath. Still cradling her restless body close to his he turned to look at the medics. "My apologies, *kyen*." He gently laid Thea down and moved out of their way, staying close to Kyrin.

Keeping a wary eye on the blue male, Corvin checked Thea's pulse and temperature. He knew that he had to be cautious and not set off Daeshen's instincts again. Ta'e'shian males would attack anyone they deemed a threat to their mate if he or she was wounded or ill. "I believe this has something to do with the conversion process. It seems to be affecting her more than it has the other women. I've pulled her samples from before the conversion and have started testing them for anything that may be causing her to react adversely."

He kept his voice low and soothing, adding a touch of lilt. Song was a very powerful tool for a healer. It would calm them, and if he sang full out it would nearly sedate them. He wiped away some blood and opened her eyes, checking the dilation of her pupils. Frowning, he listened to her. "What's she saying? It sounds familiar, but not." It reminded him of some of the ancient chants his people sang millennia ago. He hadn't heard anything similar since classes he had taken in his advanced schooling years.

Her back suddenly arched as she drew a harsh gasping breath. Slowly letting it out she eased back onto the bed, her breathing slowed and eased. A strange vibrating chant breathed from between her lips as the blood absorbed slowly back into her skin, not leaving a single trace that it had ever been present.

She sat up and opened her eyes. She was staring at something they could not see. As they watched the raw patches faded from her face, leaving faint scars. The scars began to scroll across her cheekbones; they paled and began to shimmer gently with a pale iridescence. More markings began to appear. Leaves and starbursts appeared along the back of her hands and circling her wrists. Stylized flames traced their way along her breastbones and over her shoulders. Locks of hair near her temples deepened to a blue-black that absorbed light, and finally, a setting sun blazed across her forehead and between her eyebrows. They all blinked in amazement. Those were the marks of the Gods and Goddesses. The markings faded into the same pale iridescence, matching the colors associated with each set of deities. As they continued to stare she opened her mouth and began to speak.

"Bring Our temple keepers to Us now. We would speak to them."

Kyrin and Daeshen blinked. Her soft voice had been replaced by the sound of ten people speaking as one. There was no doubt as to whom was speaking through her mouth.

Shaking, Corvin commed the temples and asked the attending asana to join them in the captain's quarters. He cut off their questions and protests and told them that they needed to come immediately.

As they waited, Thea's eyes turned to her mates. "She will be fine, no sickness harms her. Our markings had to fight to appear since they were not formed on her in the womb, as is customary." Her otherworldly gaze now turned to Corvin. "Please dismiss your assistant; Our words are not for him, and silence will be required. See to it, son of Iliria and Mo'aton."

Corvin bowed and dragged his assistant, Barik, into the other room and, after listening to several protests, ordered the man's com to remove the information. It did so and beeped when new information was ready for input. The CM edited the reason they came, leaving only the information that the captain's mate had an allergic reaction to the bath salt oils, and that it had worsened during the day to the point of her skin breaking open and bleeding. The man stared blankly for a moment before his eyes cleared. Corvin told him he was staying to speak with the captain for a few minutes and sent his assistant back to the medical area.

Returning to the bedroom quietly, he watched the trio on the bed. The men were gently clothing their mate, in preparation for the company they were expecting. Her eyes held far more knowledge than any mortals should as they watched. He suppressed a shiver; he had heard how it felt to have the eyes of the Gods touch you and always thought that it was exaggerated. Now he knew it was not so.

Several minutes passed before the door chimed softly, announcing the arrival of the temple asana. Kyrin went to meet them. He did not comment as they grumbled and muttered their way to the bedroom. Because of the time of the day the senior priests and priestesses were at the temples, and several lower level asana accompanied them.

Thea's head turned toward the door, tilting slightly as if she were listening intently to every word being said. Her eyes began to swirl with color. The white disappeared as colors began to bleed out from the center, leaving them pitch black with fans of gray, white, red and aquamarine spreading and retracting as they spun in slow circles. The deep voice of the senior priest of the Soul Temple could be heard complaining loudly about the highhanded behavior of their captain. The softer voice of the senior priestess could also be heard shushing the priest. Several other members of the asana muttered and glared.

As the asana crowded into the room their voices stilled when they caught sight of Thea. Several members paled and dropped to one knee before the bed. Swirling eyes watched them dispassionately, slowly scanning over every face, pausing here and there.

She turned to Kyrin, who had moved to stand beside Daeshen again. "Thank you for graciously allowing this invasion of your triads privacy, mates of Theadora." Ten voices echoed and rolled through the room. The vibrations made a glass bowl Thea had placed on a table sing out softly. Those disturbing eyes turned back to the group kneeling before the bed. "Our children come before Us, but in a saddening way. We do not require service of Our Chosen, the gifts are bestowed and used as seen fit. Those who have chosen to be in Our service do so with the humbling knowledge that it is for the good of all, that they will become the servants of both their God and Goddess and their people as a whole and as an individual."

Thea's hair lifted on an unseen wind. "Those who have complained about coming here, those who have allowed their station to elevate their sense of self worth, will spend one hundred twenty-six hours cleaning the temples. Nine hours for each of us insulted, for We do not place Ourselves above Our children and will not allow Our children to place themselves above others. Each of you is aware of whom you are and that We will be watching. This cleaning will be done with only rags, soap and wax. Let this remind you that your life was given in service to Ta'e and the Ta'e'sha, from the lowest to the highest."

Several of the chastened asana nodded.

"Another thing that upsets us is that you have taken human women from this planet as mates, yet, the attitude that they are less seems to be creeping among Our children." Steely eyes fixed on them. "These women have been taken from all they know and few were even asked. They have been told they are little more than breeding vessels and have been shown less and less respect as their population grows. You have taken the role of providers and protectors for them, and We expect you to treat them as the treasured gift they are. They will be the mothers of your children. They will be Our children as well. We should not have to decree that they be treated as such. See to it."

The only sound in the room was the soft, fast breathing of the occupants.

The Deities' gazes turned toward Corvin again. "Chief Medic Corvin, your tests will find that Theadora was reacting adversely to your conversion techniques because her bloodlines already carried a strain of Ta'e'shian genes. This information is not to be made public, if asked simply tell people that her change is the will of the Gods. There are several other women who have similar bloodlines, but we have halted the conversion. However, this is not what is causing the problems that the women in stasis are suffering."

Now she turned to Daeshen. "We are pleased with the work that has been completed regarding the giving of life to barren planets. The dead world of Shya and both of its moons are the first to be terraformed. We have chosen these planets because they are close to Ta'e and of sufficient sizes for our needs. One year after the terraforming is complete we will have further requests of you. Here is a list of the plants and animals we wish to have placed on Shya." Several glowing sheets of paper formed in the air before him.

Daeshen quickly accessed his com and spoke into it softly as he read the list. He sent several instructions to his personal computer. "I do not recognize all the species on the lists, my Lords and Ladies."

"Some still need to be gathered. Several of the women now aboard have useful skills that have not been noted, We suggest that you start with them for information." Another sheaf of papers appeared. "These are for the first moon, Sha'ki." Yet another sheaf of papers floated in the air, a darker color than the first two. "And these are for the third moon, Sho'bi."

"Goodbye for now, children, We will return when you have completed your tasks."

Thea's eyes closed slowly; after a moment her hand came up and she rubbed her forehead. "Ugh, I feel like I've been on a five day binge." Her eyes opened and she started. She quickly gathered the covers over her and looked around, seeing her mates she asked, "I take it the Godly Gang has finished addressing Their unruly children?"

The asana gasped at this disrespect. Several vibrating chuckles echoed in the air briefly, making Thea blush. "Well, at least they have a sense of humor." She eyed the collection in front of her. "I like your deities. They are very warm and caring, unlike several of the Gods and Goddesses worshiped on Earth. You're all very lucky."

One of the younger priests cleared his throat. He had flaming orange-red hair and golden eyes that burned with bright curiosity and warmth. "What is a five day binge, if I may ask?"

She grinned. "Oh, it's a phrase used back home. Sometimes after getting intoxicated humans wake up with an awful headache, generally the longer they are drunk the worse the headache."

He grinned back at her. "Ohhh." He was jostled several times as the asana filed out of the room. He scooted his way around the people leaving and looked at Kyrin and Daeshen for permission. When they nodded he stuck his hand out at Thea. "I'm Soren, nice to meet you, this is how you greet humans, yes?"

Thea laughed softly and shook his hand. "Nice to meet you, Soren. I'm Thea, and yes, a handshake is used to greet people in my country, but men are supposed to wait for a woman to offer her hand first."

Soren grinned again and scampered out of the room. Kyrin followed him to speak with the asana. He informed all of them that he would like to have a meeting in two hours so that they could discuss the manifestation and go over the recordings of it. After sending them on their way he went to check his mates again. Corvin was just getting ready to leave, having examined Thea while he was in the other room.

Finally having a moment of privacy, Kyrin kissed Thea and Daeshen. A soft tap on the doorway brought his head up just as he was deciding that spending the next hour with their bodies pressed against his might reassure all of them. He glared at the slim figure standing in the doorway.

"My apologies, Captain, but may I have a moment of your time, please?"

He sighed and sat on the edge of the bed. "Of course, Sya'tia, please come in and join us." He motioned toward a chair set near the bed.

Daeshen crawled onto the bed and curled behind Thea, pulling her back against his chest.

Thea stared at the woman as she slid into the room like a shadow. She was probably one of the most exotically beautiful women she had ever seen. Huge almond shaped black eyes dominated her face. The lack of any white, iris or pupil was disconcerting and very compelling at the same time. Her cheekbones were high and sharply formed, leading down to a pointed chin, giving her a very fey appearance.

Thea was reminded of some of the older paintings of faeries and other forest spirits. There was something primal and predatory about the woman. She had a haunting stillness, like that of a great cat patiently stalking its prey and waiting for that single misstep that will give it the advantage.

White hair flowed down to her hips in several loose braids. Thea noticed that she had black banding in several strands along her temples and that her hair seemed thicker than that of others. Her skin was the pale icy blue of glaciers, deep and hidden just under a layer of pure white. The faintest traces of lavender shaded her lips and cheeks. The woman was easily as tall as Kyrin and as slender as a reed. Gently rounded breasts pressed against the front of her uniform. A narrow ribcage and even smaller waist flared into curvy hips. Thea licked her lips as warmth pooled in her belly. She felt the urge to twine herself around the other woman and draw her scent deep into her nostrils, memorizing it.

Daeshen glanced down at Thea in surprise as he caught an echo of her thoughts. He sent the information to Kyrin as he studied the security officer with new interest.

They had not thought of taking a second wife, but such a strong attraction should not be ignored. He was aware of Kyrin also studying Sya'tia. They sent a wordless flow of communication to each other over their telepathic bond. Daeshen saw Sya'tia's throat vibrate slightly and knew that they were beginning to make her uncomfortable. He eased the intensity of his stare and told Kyrin, silently, to do the same.

Sya'tia slid into the chair and tried to hide her unease as all three of them studied her intently. She was used to being stared at, but it still made her uncomfortable. Being born with features that not only marked her as Chosen by the Warriors Temple, but were also considered a primitive throwback to hundreds of generations ago had always caught people's attention and made them uncomfortable. Her wrist spines trembled in their sheaths in reaction to her nervousness. She straightened her spine and reminded herself that she was good at her job and loved by her God and Goddess. Let them stare, she had much to offer should someone see past her odd looks and the fact that she always saw the world through hunter sight.

Although she would probably be forced to take her best-friend up on his offer to join his family group if she ever wanted to have children. Most men were afraid that her children would look like her.

She sighed inwardly in disappointment. She had always liked the captain and Daeshen; they always treated her as an equal and never stared or acted like she was different. It was odd, and saddening, to her that they were behaving like this now. It had not surprised her that they chose a human mate. Same sex pairing was commonly accepted among the Ta'e'sha and called *bavin*, but most eventually asked a member of the opposite sex to join them for parenting purposes, creating a mated family. While Ta'e'sha could have up to six members in a mated family they rarely had that many members. Since mating was for life it was carefully discussed before a new member was invited. Occasionally, someone approached a mated set and formally asked to be considered, but it was more common for the set to make the first overture.

Daeshen and Kyrin were a different case, however. They had been together for several years and while they occasionally had others join them in their bed they had turned down several offers from mated families and single women. It was thought that they would not ever have children and they never discussed their choices with others, so why they had turned down all those offers remained a mystery.

Sya'tia had always held the belief that they were just waiting for the right moment and person or persons. Living on the ship limited their choices of mates. Many women on their planet would turn down a mating offer that required them to live so far from their planet. Also, Kyrin being captain of the ship made it difficult for him to approach anyone.

Deciding to ignore the staring, she studied their new mate. Sya'tia liked the hint of mischief she saw. She pondered the woman's name. *Theadora, what an odd name, but it's pretty. She's going to have them running in circles!* She smiled, blinking when Thea returned it with a blinding one of her own. Looking at the three of them together made her shift uncomfortably in the chair. They all complemented each other so well.

Kyrin grinned to himself. *"We need to have a chat with our little darling, I think she just picked a fourth for us. Funny, I'd never looked at Sya'tia as a woman before, but really, she is beautiful. Either that or Theadora is having a greater impression on us than I thought. Sya'tia generally avoids getting involved with anyone, though,"* he sent to Daeshen

"I think that Thea is just making us look at things we've always taken for granted in a new way. Sya'tia is a very strong, competent woman. And I have to admit, after seeing her the way Thea does, her eyes are amazing. We are just so used to seeing hunter black as a sign of danger that we never really looked at them. I always just let my eyes slide over her."

Kyrin turned when Thea poked him in the back. "Yes, love?"

"Could you introduce us?"

"Of course. Theadora, this is Security Officer Sya'tia Osan, Sya'tia, this is our mate Theadora Auralel." As Thea scrambled off the bed to offer her hand Kyrin asked Daeshen, *"Why did I have to introduce them? She introduced herself to Soren without my help."*

"Dunno. I'll look into human etiquette, or I'll ask her later," came the reply.

Sya'tia smiled as she tentatively gripped the delicate hand Thea was holding out to her. A deep hum started to burst from her chest and she hurriedly cleared her throat. Her people had not used song to attract a mate in over three hundred years and she did not want this lovely woman to think she was completely primitive. She was a bit surprised by her strong attraction to the woman. "A pleasure to meet you, Theadora, I wish you a joyous and fruitful mating. Welcome to the *Dark Queen*."

Thea smiled shyly. "It's very nice to meet you, Sya'tia, please call me Thea. If you're an example of Ta'e'sha women

I'm going to feel very plain." She slipped back onto the bed and snuggled against Kyrin.

Sya'tia blinked in confusion. *Plain?*

Kyrin cleared his throat. "What did you want to speak with me about Sya'tia?"

She turned her attention back to her captain. "Oh, ah, well. I was thinking about the women that have been put in stasis…" Her voice trailed off as she looked at Thea again.

Sya'tia jerked her gaze back to Kyrin and kept it there. She cleared her throat nervously. "I remembered seeing at least two of the women being approached by an unmated male in the recreation room. He didn't do anything that caught my attention, but the woman who was recently put into stasis was one of the two. Then a few days ago I was watching a group of human woman talk and he approached the whole group. It made me remember the other time it had happened. He seemed to focus most of his attention on a woman with red hair. When I returned to my quarters I accessed the files of the women and looked for any other patterns. All of the women were without telepathic abilities."

Thea stiffened against Kyrin at the mention of telepathic abilities. Kyrin absently rubbed her arm.

"I also noted that each of the women were said to have strong personalities, but reacted favorably to mating with our men. You asked us to report any patterns we may have noticed, so I came to speak with you about it."

Kyrin pondered her words for a few minutes. "This is actually very interesting information, did you identify the man and the women at the table?"

She nodded, taking a small holoreader out of her pocket and giving it to him. "I haven't been able to determine if he knew the other women yet. The woman he was speaking to the other night is very similar in personality to the others. According to her files her mate actually spent several months wooing her before she was brought aboard. He offered her the choice of staying on Earth or coming with him"

He nodded as he accessed the information. After studying it for a minute he looked up. "Are you absolutely certain this is the right man?"

She nodded.

Kyrin ordered the computer to contact CM Corvin and request that he com back in a private area. Afterward he requested a screen along the far wall.

A few moments later Corvin's image appeared before them. "Yes, Captain?"

"Doctor Corvin, are you in a private area and alone right now?"

Corvin frowned. "Yes. I'm in my office and no one is with me at the moment."

"Have you located a human psychologist yet?"

The doctor nodded. "Yes, we located one and another woman who worked in a crisis center. We were going to bring one of the women out of stasis today. I have two female doctors and a female aide who will be present. We'll see if Thea is right, hopefully not having men present will give us the chance to help these women."

Kyrin nodded. "Good, let me know as soon as possible what the outcome is." He rubbed a hand across his face. "Your aide, Barik, has been identified as being in the company of two of the women before their episodes started. Can you think of any reason he would have for approaching them? He has declined selecting a mate from among the humans."

Corvin stilled. "No, offhand, I can't think of a reason. But, then, I have no control over what happens outside his working hours. He seems fascinated by humans, but he also avoids them when they came to medical." He tapped a finger on his desk. "Just what are you implying, Captain?"

"He was also seen in the company of another woman a few days ago. She fits the same pattern as the others. Strong, non-telepathic, petite, and happy with her husband. Right now, I'm withholding any judgment or actions until the women in stasis can be interviewed. But this is also something I cannot ignore. I'm putting a guard on the woman until we find out if Thea's theory is correct."

The doctor nodded. "Yes, I understand. If you'll excuse me, I think I'll find something for him to do out of the office for the next few days while we conduct the interviews." He looked deeply troubled.

Stopping just before he blanked the screen, he spoke, not looking up, "Kyrin… If you are right…" He looked up and took a deep breath. "It's going to be a mess. Barik is a son of one of the royal clans. And the repercussions of a medic doing something like this… It's going to shake everyone's faith in doctors. I'd like to keep it as quiet as possible, but I don't know how we can."

Kyrin nodded. "I know. I'm working on that, Corvin."

Corvin nodded tiredly.

Sya'tia cleared her throat, both men looked at her. "Captain, whoever is responsible for this, perhaps they should be taken before the High asana, then, regardless of identity, the trial will be indisputable. I believe that, in any case, this should be made public. We must show that the human women will be treated the same as the women of our race. To hush it up and downplay it demeans the victims."

Thea shook her head. "I don't disagree with the trial, Sya'tia, but I think the women should be asked about the publicity. Rape is... More than merely an invasion and having others witness a very public trial may make them feel even more violated."

Daeshen sighed. "It's a moot point right now. We need the interviews first. We'll worry about details after that."

Kyrin nodded in agreement. "Sya'tia, please have some guards look after the woman you identified. Ask them to be as unobtrusive as possible. I'll speak to her and her mate after the interviews are completed if it's needed."

Sya'tia nodded crisply as she stood. "Of course, sir. I'll handle it." She smoothed her hands down her uniform and bowed, preparing to leave.

Thea scrambled off the bed and took the other woman's hand. "It was so nice to meet you. Would you like to join us for dinner this evening? We could watch a movie afterwards?" She waited anxiously for the response.

Sya'tia cleared her throat nervously. She looked at Kyrin, who smiled and nodded encouragingly.

Daeshen also nodded. "That would be fun, Sya'tia. Thea was telling me about creatures called vampires and we are going to watch a movie about them tonight. There is one in particular called 'Dracula' that features prominently in their mythology and the movie is about him. And she says the man playing that part is a 'smokin hottie'." He grinned engagingly. "We are having *shoomoe...*" he enticed. It was well known that it was one of her favorite dishes. She always had a plateful when the galley made the mix of crisp fried vegetables and paper-thin fish fillets.

Sya'tia swayed between yes and no. She wanted to come, but was startled by the invitation. "Shoomoe?" She bit her lip. The movie sounded intriguing, too. She had watched one human movie and not understood half of what was going on. Maybe it would be more enjoyable with Thea there to explain things.

Thea nodded eagerly. "And popcorn with the movie!"

She smiled hesitantly. "All right. It sounds like fun. And I love shoomoe."

Thea laughed happily. "This is so cool! I'll see you tonight! Don't forget." She beamed up at the taller woman. Noticing that she was petting her hand she blushed and dropped it. "Sorry. I pet things. Let me know if I annoy you."

Sya'tia smiled down at the charming creature her captain had chosen. "I don't mind. I like it." She blushed when she caught Daeshen and Kyrin smiling at her like they knew something she did not. She left as quickly and gracefully as she could.

Thea looked at the now closed door wistfully. She turned and looked at her husbands. "She's really nice, isn't she?" Her brow creased in sudden concern. "I didn't make her uncomfortable, did I?"

Daeshen smiled as he lounged against Kyrin's side. "No, sweetheart, I don't think it was that." He patted the space beside them. "Come sit with us."

She climbed back onto the bed.

Kyrin cleared his throat. "You seemed to be, hmmm, attracted to her."

She blushed.

Daeshen grinned.

"Um, yeah, I guess so," she murmured softly. Suddenly the weave of the fabric the sheets were made of was fascinating to her. She picked at it with a fingernail, not looking at either of them.

"Do you want us to consider her for marriage?"

Her head shot up and she stared at Kyrin with wide eyes. "Wh-what?"

The men smiled.

Daeshen pulled her closer to them. "Would you like to consider her for a wife? We have no objections. Sya'tia is a wonderful person."

Thea blinked. "Uhh, well, umm, you want to marry her? How many wives can you guys have?" She felt very confused. They wanted another wife? Did they regret choosing her?

Kyrin rubbed her back. "We can have up to five spouses, love, a family group of six is accepted. We hadn't planned on having anyone else added to ours, but it's hard to ignore an attraction as strong as there was between the two of you. I thought that Sya'tia was going to start singing to catch your attention at any moment."

"But I'm not gay," she mumbled softly.

He leaned closer to hear her. "What was that?"

She glared at him. "I said I'm not gay."

"What does how happy you are have to do with it?" He looked perplexed.

"Not gay! *Gay!*" If anything they looked even more bewildered.

"Uhh…" Daeshen ventured uncertainly.

"One who prefers lovers of their own sex," she gritted out. She could almost see a light bulb go on over their heads.

"Ohhh…"they chorused.

Kyrin smirked. "We are well aware that you like men, love." Daeshen snickered. "But, that doesn't mean you can't enjoy the attentions of a woman, as well. We enjoy men and women. There's nothing wrong with that." He cast her a sly smile. "And I don't think you mind watching two men together, either."

She blushed again, and then sighed. It seemed that her face was destined to be red around the two of them. "No, I don't mind," she muttered.

Kyrin pulled her into his lap. "So, then we come back to the original point of this conversation: would you like us to consider Sya'tia?" He nibbled on her ear, smiling when she shivered.

She nodded hesitantly. "Yes, I guess so. Do you both want to consider her, too?"

He nodded against her throat, where his mouth had wandered. "Yes, we wouldn't mind at all. We've both known her for years and like her. And, you're right, she is very beautiful. Just not in the way we are used to seeing. It took you coming into our life and meeting her to open our eyes."

She pulled away and looked from one to the other. "What do you mean 'not the way you're used to'? And how did I make you look at her differently?"

Daeshen pondered her question for a minute before he answered her. "Sya'tia...does not have features that are common among our people any longer. In fact, many people have said that she looks like a primitive throwback."

Thea frowned, thinking of the lovely woman she had just met.

"Also, her eyes are full black. All of our eyes can turn black but it only happens if we sense a threat or are hunting at the time. We have a second pair of black lids inside our eyes that change our sight so that we can also track heat signatures. It's very unusual for her to have her eyes always in hunter mode. It makes people shy away from her because when we see someone's eyes bleed black we start looking for something dangerous near us."

"Oh," she said softly. Looking up, she caught them exchanging a look. "What else?" She sighed.

"Umm... Well, she's also a Chosen of the Warriors Temple. That makes her very dangerous. She has hinged fangs inside her mouth that contain paralytic venom that affects voluntary muscles. There are spines in her wrists that contain a deadly neurotoxin. She is also stronger and better trained martially than the rest of the populace, excepting the other Chosen of the Warriors."

Thea gulped. "Oh."

Daeshen smiled and picked up her hand, gently kissing her fingers. "On the other hand... She's very sweet and shy. She spends most of her time alone and is very good at her job."

She smiled and nodded.

Kyrin hugged her tightly. "We'll see how things go this evening, there's no use in getting ahead of ourselves." He kissed them each again. "And I have to go now. I have to meet the asana. Stay out of trouble."

Daeshen traced the marks on her cheeks lightly with a thumb. "Poor love. It's been one thing after another, hasn't it?"

She smiled and tugged him closer. "Yeah, well, I can think of something that might make up for some of it." She nipped the tip of his nose.

He grinned and tumbled her back into the pillows. "Oh, really? Well, far be it from me to deny you..."

* * *

Elsewhere...

"It is too late to worry if we are doing the right thing, Shaysha. We have already acted and must continue to do so." Byasuen darted across the star filled void with a flick of her tail and laid her hand against her sister-Goddess's cheek. "It was also necessary to show our full support of these women and set an example for our children --"

"And it's just too bad you didn't speak to her parents first, darling sister," said a low, husky voice irritably from behind the ten deities. "I do not appreciate my daughters being stolen from my arms and I care even less for them becoming the mouths of other deities."

They turned to greet the two cloaked and hooded figures who had joined them.

Both figures pushed their hoods down and glared at the Ta'e Lithen. The man and woman seemed to age and become young again as the time passed, their hair was a dark gold that deepened to the rich brown of fertile earth before fading to a snowy white and beginning the cycle again; only their eyes stayed the same, the rich black-brown of fertile earth.

Kashka smiled dryly. "Nice entrance, sister, brother. Although I suppose knocking is hard since we don't have a door. And what names are you two going by this millennium?"

"Thea refers to us as Gaia and Skye, so that will work. Our children don't generally call us by name. Most simply use Lord and Lady." Gaia seated herself in midair and crossed her legs.

Skye shook his head and leaned against her. "Are you two ever going to get along? I swear The Great One was going to send you to your rooms at the last mixer when you two got into it and knocked over the punch bowl."

Kashka rolled her eyes. "That was, what? Two thousand years ago? When one of our brothers sent his kid down to earth on a field trip? Besides, she said my ass was so fat she could see spaces between my scales."

Mo'aton coughed to hide a snicker. "I remember him. 'I don't need a name, my followers call me the Almighty.' He was arrogant, even for a God. Is he still around or did the Great One eat him with sauce?"

Gaia grunted. "Oh, he's still around. And he hates the rest of us; I don't know how many of our other sibling's children his followers have killed in his name. I have a feeling he'll go the Greek Way on us, if the Great One doesn't Atlantis him instead."

All twelve shuddered, remembering the Great One's anger at those sets of Gods and Goddesses.

Skye flopped down on the easy chair that manifested beside him and popped open the beer that appeared in his hand. "Okay, subject change. Back to our sibling rivalries. Yer kids snatched our girls. At least nine of my baby girls are on this ship alone. And two of 'em have been having the twitches trying to figure out how to call a circle and elements when east ain't east."

Gaia sighed. "At least you haven't heard the freaked thoughts of 'what's artificial gravity gonna do to my period?' and 'I'M HAVING AN ALIEN BABY!' One of them is starting to review the Weekly World News in her head and wonder how much of it is true."

Iliria winced. "We had no intention of any of this happening."

"Well, that didn't stop you from using Thea, did it?" Skye slurped down a slug of beer. He set the can down with a thump and glared at them again. "Do you have any idea how fragile she is right now? Do you realize that it won't take much more to break her?" His face hardened. "Our daughters being among your children gives us a doorway that was closed when the Great One took you and your children away from Earth. And we will use it to protect them. And you may want to consider what other doors have been opened."

Gaia nodded in agreement. "Thea may be your voice, because you're right, it's needed. Your children will not fully accept them otherwise. We will let her know that we approve, and are proud of her faith in us. Meeting you didn't shake her belief in us one little bit. But..." She smiled evilly. "Your children need a little lesson in respect. Don't worry, though, we'll handle it."

Skye smirked.

Both figures faded out with a little wave.

Byasuen thunked her head against her mate's chest. "Lovely... Just lovely... Those two can be as cruel as their winter aspects; what do you think they are going to do?"

Chapter Nine

Thea and Sya'tia gasped as the handsome, dark haired man snarled, showing his gruesome fangs and dove for the bared throat of the fair damsel who stared rapturously upwards. A trickle of blood oozed from the corner of his mouth and down the alabaster column of her throat.

Thea reached for another handful of popcorn from the bowl cradled between them. She munched on the crunchy treat, not paying any attention to the kernels that dropped into her lap as she stared at the screen, completely enthralled.

The fair damsel collapsed gracefully to the ground and the vampire threw his head back and laughed darkly.

Sya'tia snagged her own handful of popcorn and nibbled at it daintily. "When does the hunter show up?" she asked, licking her fingers. "These vampires would be interesting prey, so quick and strong. A true challenge." She wiggled deeper into the gel seat and stretched out her legs before grabbing another handful of popcorn.

Thea munched thoughtfully for a moment. "He'll show up soon, I think. They are usually about five seconds too late." She wiped her hands on a napkin and stood. "Want some more soda?" She picked up both glasses when the woman nodded in assent. Turning, she tilted her head inquiringly at her husbands. They both shook their heads.

Sya'tia had been hesitant when she had first arrived and had been a bit bemused by Thea. The smaller women practically hummed with energy. She was the perfect complement for Kyrin's somber authority and Daeshen's exacting nature. But, she had quickly relaxed under Thea's friendly attention.

Sya'tia gasped as the vampire hunter dashed flamboyantly into the room, brandishing a stake. He surveyed the scene and targeted the vampire with a steely eye. Sya'tia wiggled in her seat in anticipation. The vampire hissed at the man and leapt away from the fallen woman. He called out a mocking challenge to the hunter and jumped out a nearby window with a dramatic swirl of his cape. She hissed in displeasure. The hunter ran to the window and stared out. Nothing could be seen but withered tree branches and scraggly wisps of fog.

Thea darted back in, carrying the now filled glasses and plopped back down beside Sya'tia. "What'd I miss?" she asked breathlessly.

Sya'tia glowered. "The vampire jumped out the window!" Her voice was filled with indignation as she watched the hunter check the unconscious woman.

Thea waved a hand. "They always do that. Sneaky weasels."

The movie progressed.

Both women cheered loudly as the hunter triumphantly drove the stake through the heart of the now vanquished vampire.

A lively discussion ensued afterwards. Daeshen asked Thea questions about her world's mythology while Kyrin and Sya'tia plotted a new virtual reality scenario based on the movie. Thea suggested they watch more vampire movies before they put the game together. Sya'tia liked that idea and borrowed several of Thea's novels to read as well.

They made plans to watch another movie the next evening. Thea suggested something different, so that no one became tired of vampires.

Kyrin smiled down at her. "What movie do you suggest, love?"

"*Warlock*," she replied promptly. "Julian Sands was fantastic in it! Sya'tia seems to like horror movies, and it's one of my favorites." She beamed up at him.

Sya'tia bounced in her seat a little. "Oh, yes! That was so much fun! I would like to see more! I will bring dinner tomorrow, if that is all right?" She smiled shyly.

"Sounds good, I'll make crispy treats for movie snacks." The women wandered off, heads together as they made plans.

Daeshen grinned. "That went well, don't you think?" His mate nodded solemnly, but his eyes held a distinct twinkle. They both followed the women.

Thea had dug out a carton of ice cream and was scooping it into bowls when the men joined them. Sya'tia paused in her lively dissertation of how the virtual reality decks worked to smile at them both.

She blushed faintly when Kyrin winked at her. She was still a bit bemused by Thea, but found the woman charming and humorous and very welcoming. She took the bowl that was offered to her, still listening to Thea chatter happily and the men's deeper responses. She eyed the name marks tattooed on Kyrin's throat wistfully. Both men had touched their marks unconsciously throughout the evening. Their obvious pleasure in them and their mated status made her yearn for a family of her own.

A soft chime announced someone at the door. Kyrin went to answer.

Daeshen settled himself in the chair next to Sya'tia and nibbled at the brown goop on his spoon with a cautious expression. Evidently he decided it was good. He dug his spoon back in with more enthusiasm. Sya'tia grinned at him.

Kyrin returned with Corvin in tow. They exchanged greetings. Thea made him a bowl of ice cream without asking, and placed it in front of him before taking a seat for herself.

Corvin cleared his throat and poked his spoon around without tasting the ice cream. "We have finished the first interview."

The room fell quiet as four pairs of bright eyes fixed on him with unnerving intensity.

"The woman admits to being raped. She described exactly how she was drugged, taken from a public area, and raped. She woke up back in her own cabin with all of her clothing back on and no memory of being taken back." He looked up from his bowl. "When we asked her if she could describe her assailant she began to have seizures. We sedated her to stop them, but we are not going to put her back in stasis. I spoke with the counselors; they are going to begin therapy and try to avoid speaking of what the assailant looks like until we can determine the cause of the seizures. It may be the stress, but I'm not sure. She doesn't have a history of epilepsy in her medical files."

"We will interview the other women tomorrow. I spoke with the Balance asana. They have not noticed any unusual mental activity. As soon as the women recover enough the asana will come to medical and try to help spiritually." He rubbed his temples wearily and slid a holoreader to Kyrin. "Here are the transcripts of the interview. Maybe we can get something off the security logs from the times she gave us."

Sya'tia frowned thoughtfully. "I will have them checked. We found several times in the logs that seemed to be scrambled. The computer didn't report it because they all fell within the parameters of acceptable time loss. I will crosscheck the static against the time she gave you. Perhaps we can download the information from her cerebcom."

Kyrin nodded and had his cerebcom download a copy of the transcript into a holoreader in Sya'tia's quarters. "You should have a copy of the transcripts by the time you return to your quarters this evening, Sya'tia."

The conversation faded around Thea as she drew into herself. She had managed to forget that little comment about telepathy during the course of the evening. *Telepathic? And what the hell is a cerebcom?* The information that a small computer had been implanted in her brain, as well as its location and capabilities, floated through her thoughts, unbidden. She was absolutely certain that she had no idea where this information came from. Her lungs tightened in her chest as the implications of telepathy and that little scrap of knowledge she should not have rolled through her mind. *Maybe that's why I'm accepting this so well... Have they been messing with my mind? How much of me really is me?*

How powerful are they? She slipped out of the room unnoticed. This was something she needed to think about first. Then, she would approach her husbands. Or kill 'em. Well, maybe, just a good maiming.

* * *

Kyrin bid their guests goodnight two hours later and sealed the door. He turned to Daeshen and sighed. Halfway through the discussion with Corvin and Sya'tia they had both developed low, throbbing aches in their temples.

They exchanged grimaces and started looking for their mate.

"Why is she so upset?" Daeshen muttered

"Your guess is as good as mine," was the mumbled reply.

They peered cautiously around the door of the library. Laser hot gray eyes lanced them from over the top of a book. "Go away," was growled from behind the aforementioned book.

Daeshen scooted around Kyrin and into the room. He approached her slowly. "What's wrong, love?" He quickly ducked when she threw her book at him.

She glared at them both. "What's wrong? Oh gee, where to start? You're telepathic and didn't see fit to mention that… You stuck a piece of metal in my brain and didn't find the time to bring that up either! It's dumping information in my head that makes no sense and I can only wonder what else was done to me." She glowered at Kyrin, who was slinking into the room. "I'm tattooed and pierced like a biker chick and shaved like a porn star. I got married without being asked." She continued to count off her complaints on her fingers. "I got to channel your deities. Hell, my own deities don't talk to me as much as yours do!" She looked around for something else to throw.

Daeshen blinked. "Nothing more was done to you. All of us have cerebcoms, love. They make life easier aboard the ship. The only difference between yours and ours is that it gives you more information about our culture. It's set so that if you think of a question it will try to answer it, if the information is in our database."

She glared at them. She had managed to discover that for herself while the men were busy. But much of the information that had come flooding in at her tentative attempts to use the cerebcom had confused her and given her a headache, which had served the purpose of irritating her all the more.

Kyrin spoke softly to her. "You are worried that we have tampered with your mind telepathically, aren't you? That you may not be the same person you were before you met us."

She nodded, looking away.

Kyrin thought about that for a few moments. He rubbed the back of his neck, carefully choosing his words. "We could tell you that, ethically, we would not do such a thing. We could also tell you that such tampering is very difficult, if not impossible, to do. This is because the person you are, or anyone is, begins to form from the moment of your birth, and in the case of a telepathic person, even before birth."

Daeshen nodded in agreement. "This is true, love." He scooted a little closer when no further projectiles were aimed in his direction.

Kyrin rubbed his chin as he continued, "But I believe that you would have a great deal of difficulty believing us right now. I would imagine that you are feeling that we have betrayed you and your trust?"

She nodded, listening, but not quite ready to give up being pissed off at their high-handedness.

Daeshen smiled and patted her knee. "Then you should wait and speak with someone else? Perhaps one of the asana? They would be able to explain the abilities inherent in our race to you better than we could."

"Your race," she growled softly, suddenly furious again. "Your race can kiss my ass. Where the hell do you people get off? You seem to think you have the right to do this to us. Like we are some lowly beings that should be grateful that you deign to notice us and make our decisions for us! How dare you?"

Both men winced, hearing her say the things they had thought.

Thea stood and started pacing; finally giving vent to the things that had been roaming around in her brain. She was starting to feel like her brain was a hamster in a wheel. A lot of effort and not going anywhere.

Daeshen fell back, looking up at her with a startled expression.

"I think I've been a pretty good sport about this! But enough is enough!" She advanced on Kyrin and poked him in the chest, following when he backed up with a slightly panicked expression. "Oh, sure, you all come off as peaceful, humble little scientists! NOT! What, you think they'd get away with this kind of crap on Star Trek? HELL NO! Spock would have been all over Kirk like a bad rash in August!" she snarled up in his face.

Kyrin exchanged a bewildered look with Daeshen, who was still sitting on his ass staring at Thea like she was a mouse that had suddenly grown fangs and claws and launched at his jugular. He cleared his throat. "Now, darling…"

"Don't you 'now, darling' me, mister!" She growled again. "You are not nice people! You try, but fail. Oh sure, some of the women were asked, but it's not like they had all the information before they made their decision, did they? You all smile so sweetly and say 'come away with me, I love you, I need you, you are everything I ever wanted.' Shyeah right! Just forgot to mention that little DNA conversion-get-yer-ass-shaved-never-see-your-family-or-friends-again thing, right? And THEN you wonder why we are pissed off and resentful, and oh, maybe, just a little DEPRESSED!" She panted, hands fisted at her sides. "And don't even get me started about waking up naked and tied up like a bondage queen? Oh, aren't you two Mr. Sensitivity?"

Color flooded Kyrin's cheeks. "Uhh…" he ventured intelligently.

Daeshen winced. "We thought you liked that stuff," he mumbled.

Kyrin shook his head franticly when Thea turned on the other man like a furious snake.

"Oh yeah! Every woman dreams of being kidnapped and waking up TERRIFIED while two strange men grope her!" she screeched and swatted at the side of his head, missing when he quickly scooted back from her. She glared at him when he jumped up and darted behind Kyrin. He peered at her from over the other man's shoulder.

Thea glowered at them. They were staring at her with bewildered, wary eyes and comical expressions of absolute dismay. Her lips twitched.

They backed up another step.

Kyrin stumbled over Daeshen as he stepped back. He eyed his furious little mate, thoughts racing through his brain. "We don't like it either, Theadora. But, you have to understand our side of things --"

"No, I don't, actually," came the sneered response.

Daeshen sighed and rested his forehead on Kyrin's shoulder. "We do love you, mate. And we have waited for you all our lives. We are more sorry than you can know that we could not court you and allow you time to know us and accept us." He felt Kyrin nod in agreement. "Our people are desperate, Thea, and you know that desperation can bring out the worst in anyone. Please, just give us a chance; give our marriage a chance. We are trying to make it better. We are doing everything we can." He looked up at her with sad eyes.

Thea felt her expression soften. They looked so sad it broke her heart.

Both men slid toward the door. "We will leave you to your thoughts, my dear," Kyrin told her softly. "Come to us when you are ready," he continued as they began to slink from the room.

Thea brooded silently. She had been ready to have a rip-snorting fight complete with screaming, yelling and more than one thrown object. Instead she felt like she had been kicking puppies in front of children. She glowered at her lap. *Men suck.*

Picking up her book she went to her workroom. After a few minutes of questioning her cerebcom and sorting through the responses she managed to lock the door. A few more minutes of struggling produced the soft strains of Loreena McKennitt's haunting ballads. She flopped down on her stool and glared at the ceiling balefully.

Dragging several pieces of heavy cloth out of boxes she laid them out in a makeshift pallet. A few skeins of yarn wrapped with another cloth formed a pillow. Surveying her bed with satisfaction she smiled. The quiet and feeling of privacy soothed her ragged nerves. Grabbing her book she stretched out to read until she was sleepy. *I need to take my mind off this for a while. Just a little while.*

Finally she turned out the light and closed her eyes, trying not to think about her life and the men who were becoming so important to it.

Chapter Ten

Thea woke slowly and sat up. She groaned softly at the stiffness in her muscles and cautiously stretched to loosen them. Last night's "discussion" with her husbands was still swishing around in her sleep-hazed mind. She made a mental note to herself to find a bed for her workroom since this was probably only one of the several times she was going to find herself needing a retreat from her darlings over the course of their lives.. *And I'm not going to sleep on the floor every time they do something stupid or I need some time to myself.*

Her belly cramped with sudden hunger. She licked her lips, distracted from her pout and glower session. *Fish. Mmm... And some eggs, too.* She unlocked the door to her workroom, heading for the dining area to order a large breakfast of sushi with a side of smelt roe, eggs over easy, watermelon pickles, and milk.

While she waited for it to come she slipped into the bedroom and quietly pulled out some fresh clothing to wear. She glowered at the warm tangle of limbs curled in the center of their bed. The hubbies certainly looked comfy. *Men suck.* For a few blissful moments she contemplated a nice, cold glass of water right in the center of them. Setting aside her thoughts with a sigh she went to take a quick shower before her breakfast arrived.

* * *

Kyrin yawned and stumbled into the kitchen for a glass of water. His nose wrinkled at the unpleasant odor that assailed it. He looked at his wife blearily. She ignored him and continued enthusiastically crunching her way through a pile of fragrant white-green cubes between bites of what looked like cloudy white mush. He shuddered and didn't ask; he simply got his glass of water and stumbled to the bathing area.

He made sure the door slid completely shut behind him. He didn't want the smell following him.

For good measure he grabbed a bottle of deodorant and sprayed the room liberally. *What was she eating that smelled so awful?* He wasn't going to ask though.

She might make him try it

Thea chewed on her pickle slowly and added a few more lines on to the sketch she was working on. She watched Kyrin scoot out of the room from the corner of her eye and smirked. *Nothing like the aroma of fish eggs and sweet pickles first thing in the morning to start your day off right!* Humming to herself more cheerfully now, she slurped up another swallow of her milk and thought about what she wanted to do with her day. *And few things make a bad mood better faster than sharing it with an innocent victim!*

After finishing her breakfast she stacked her plates and ordered tea and some of the seaweed biscuits the men preferred for their own breakfast to be delivered in approximately thirty minutes. That completed, she locked herself in her workroom again to work on her tapestry.

Several hours later she peered into Daeshen's office. It was empty. She did the sneaky ninja stalk to the bedroom. Empty. She scampered silently to the door of the bathing area. *Score!* She heard the faint sounds of splashing. More sneaky ninja stalking to the door of their suite. After a brief triumph dance she strolled down the hall. *Okay, part one complete! Now, if I can just figure out where Sya'tia is...* She consulted with the cerebcom briefly. It would not give her detailed information for privacy reasons, as it was Sya'tia's off day. Mentally shrugging she decided to explore a bit.

The sheer size of the ship soon overwhelmed her. The crew and passengers all seemed to be very friendly. Although they rarely paused to speak to her, everyone had a smile. She stopped by Sya'tia's cabin, having asked directions from a crewman passing by, but there was no response when she pressed the "doorbell."

Biting her lip she paused at a loss for what she should do now. She decided to go back to her quarters, watch a movie and wait till that evening and drag her friend off when she came for dinner. Heading back the way she came, Thea paused uncertainly at an intersection. *Which way did I come?* She requested directions from her cerebcom and staggered against the wall at the unexpected flood of information that cascaded through her mind. Instead of identifying a single path it had sent all routes she might possibly take. She rubbed her forehead. *Ow.* Sighing, she took a hall and hoped for the best.

* * *

Soren paused in his industrious waxing of a small wooden sculpture of Shaysha, Goddess of spiritual and mental balance. A faint twinge of distress whispered through his mind. He concentrated on the feeling and it drifted away. Shrugging, he went back to what he was doing. He had decided to spend a few hours doing the same activities as those of his order who had been chastened to remind himself of who and what he served.

Mentally returning to his meditations he lovingly rubbed the oily cloth over the wood, removing dust and buffing it to a high shine. Humming softly, he let the peace of the temple saturate his senses.

The rich scent of the polishing oils, and the soft strains of Ta'e'sha song lightly tickled his ears. The dark wood paneling the walls seemed to hold shadows as close as a lover and whispered secrets teasingly just out of his hearing.

A few minutes later the twinge returned, a bit stronger this time. Frowning, he set aside the now cleaned statue and followed the sensation.

It led him out of the temple and along several corridors until he was walking through an area of unoccupied cabins. The feeling of distress grew stronger and his pace picked up in reaction to it.

Turning a corner he almost tripped over Thea. She was slumped on the floor against the wall with her knees drawn up under her chin and looked near tears. The sensation faded down to a low hum in the back of his mind. He had arrived at his destination.

Thea looked up and smiled with relief. "Hi, Soren. Can you help me find my way back home?"

Soren sat down next to her. "Hi, Thea. I can help you go back home." The small woman looked relieved, but the distress did not fade completely. "Is there anything else wrong?"

Thea rested her chin on her knees again, making no move to get up. "Lots of stuff. I kinda feel like I'm playing blind man's bluff, but everyone else left after spinning me."

He drew up his knees and watched her. "What's blind man's bluff?"

She smiled faintly. "It's a game children play. One person is blindfolded and spun in circles until they are dizzy. Then they are let go and have to try and catch one of the other children."

He thought about that for a bit.

Thea gnawed on a fingernail.

"That doesn't sound like a lot of fun," he said at last. In fact it sounded downright nauseating.

She smiled. "It's not. Well, it is when you're a kid, but when you get older you usually just feel queasy."

"Why do you feel that way?"

She frowned thoughtfully, looking down at the floor. "Well, I woke up here and found out I was married, whether I liked it or not. And to two men, too. That's just weird and illegal where I come from. Then, I find out they are telepathic, so hey, maybe they messed with my mind so that I would accept all of this more easily. Which is creepy, I mean, how would you feel if you had a bunch of strangers crawling around in your mind doing whatever the hell they wanted to? Digging through your memories like they were your underwear drawer?"

His nose wrinkled.

She continued, "And don't even get me started on them sticking a computer in my head. *Then*, they don't even bother telling me about it let alone how to work the damn thing. I'm surprised I haven't fried my own brain." Her monologue continued as she listed all the travails she had gone through in the past few days.

Soren listened quietly. He had never thought about any of this from the point of view of the women. Things that were completely normal, honorable and expected to him were foreign and frightening to them. The marriage tattoos. Body piercing was common. The ethics of telepathy were well established and well known. Cerebcoms were common, even among people who were not living on ships. There was not much he could say about them being taken without their permission, but maybe he could help her with some of her other concerns.

He waited until she had wound down to pensive silence. "Hmmm, why don't you come back to the temple with me for a little while, Thea? Maybe some of the older asana and I can help you sort this out and answer some of your questions."

She shrugged dispiritedly, but stood when he did. "I probably shouldn't stay too long; Daeshen doesn't know I'm gone."

"I'll com the captain and let him know where you are."

He led her back toward the more populated area of the ship and tried to think of the best way to explain things to her. Clearing his throat, he began with the subject he thought might be the one bothering her most.

"Our race has always been telepathic. We believe it's because we evolved under water. We do have a spoken language we use when we are swimming; it is similar to that used by the dolphins and whales on your planet, but it's a bit like yelling when you want to whisper. It echoes all over till everyone hears it, so we generally used it when we were addressing a large group of people." He paused again, trying to sort his thoughts. "Although it was hilarious the time my friend Kairn whispered 'nice scales, baby' to one of the girls in school. She slapped him and the whole class made fun of him for a month."

He came back to his original subject after Thea giggled softly. "Telepathic speech develops about three months into the mother's pregnancy. Our parents teach us to focus our thoughts so that we aren't sending to all and sundry after we are born. From the time we begin our education we are taught what is acceptable."

Thea listened intently, watching him from the corner of her eye. She waited expectantly when he paused again.

Soren stared at the ground as they walked slowly toward the entrance of the temple. He decided to wait to finish the discussion until they were inside and he could ask a senior asana to join them.

He held the door open for her and motioned for her to sit down at one of the small circular areas made for people to sit while they waited to be attended by the asana. "Wait here, Thea. I'll go com the captain and see if a senior asana is free to talk with us." He gave her an embarrassed grin. "I'm still new at this and I don't want to bungle it and confuse you even more."

She smiled wanly and settled into the seat. "Okay."

He disappeared through a door that was placed toward the back of the room.

She looked around curiously. The room was shaped like a wide wedge. Warm, dark red wood covered the walls and silky gray fabric hung from ceiling to floor at even intervals. The curving benches at each of the meditation areas were covered with the same gray fabric. She ran her palm over it. It felt like a heavy raw silk.

There was an archway in one wall that led into a similar looking room. The only difference was that the fabric in that room was a deep, vibrant aquamarine. She turned and looked behind her. There was another door, leading into a room decorated with red.

She looked back down at the bench and rubbed her finger along the wood. It was sanded smooth and felt warm and almost velvety. Hearing soft voices she looked up. Soren was speaking softly with a woman in a gray jumpsuit similar to his.

Thea inspected the woman as they approached her. She had dark lavender hair that fell around her shoulders. It was twisting itself into several knots, creating an intricate design along the back of her head and neck. Her eyes were a shade or two lighter, and seemed to smile warmly. She was obviously older, but the sense of inner stillness she had about her created the impression that she was ageless.

The sight of them together made her smile. Soren, with his bright orange-red hair and friendly personality made her think of an exuberant puppy bouncing along the side of his patient and sweet tempered dam.

Soren assisted the older priestess into a seat across from Thea and then sat down next to her. "Thea, this is Senior Priestess Kyaness. Kyaness, this is Theadora Auralel."

Thea smiled and offered her hand. "It's a pleasure to meet you, Kyaness."

The older woman smiled. She took Thea's hand and turned it palm up, stroking her hand from the inside of Thea's elbow to her wrist. "Hello, Thea." She released Thea. "That is a formal greeting among the Ta'e'sha. Soren tells me that you have questions regarding our culture, I would be happy to help you."

Chapter Eleven

Foam burst from the woman's mouth as her back arched sharply against the chair she sat in. Her nails scrabbled against the arms of her chair. Tortured gasps issued from her throat.

Corvin launched himself from his seat. He pulled her to the floor and stuck a heavy rubber plug into her mouth. Once he was sure she was not in danger of swallowing her tongue he pressed a syringe against the side of her neck and administered a muscle relaxant.

Within moments the spasms eased and her body relaxed against the floor. She stared up at the ceiling and panted. Tears leaked from the corners of her unblinking eyes. Her body shook with another, less forceful, seizure.

Reba, the rape counselor who was conducting the interview with Corvin, gently stroked the woman's forehead. "You'll be all right, Sara, please don't be frightened." She exchanged a look with the doctor. Motioning with her head, she urged him to back away from the woman.

Corvin nodded and eased himself slowly away from Sara's prone form. He mentally requested that her physical information be downloaded to his office from her cerebcom. He had every intention of going over it with a fine toothcomb to see if he could pinpoint exactly what was causing the seizures. They were happening far too conveniently for his peace of mind. There had to be something he was missing. *Hypnosis maybe? No... Not everyone is susceptible to hypnosis.*

Reba helped the woman stand on unsteady legs. Wrapping an arm around her waist she helped her walk to the bed that had been set up in the room. Sara had not wanted to go home to her mate after she woke up. She had asked for a few days to herself first, although, she wanted to see him before she retired to sleep.

He quietly exited the room, knowing that Reba would join him as soon as Sara was settled and her mate joined her.

* * *

Thea smiled tentatively at her husbands. Kyrin was looking down at her sternly while Daeshen was giving her a kicked puppy look. She winced mentally. *Great, they act like a couple of asses and somehow I'm the bad girl.*

Kyrin grabbed her wrist and yanked her hard against his chest. His stern expression softened after a moment and he bent his head to brush his mouth against hers tenderly. "Welcome home, love. Next time you decide to go exploring please let us know first." His hands slipped around her waist and stroked her lower back lazily.

Daeshen scooted closer and bent to press a small kiss under her ear. "Don't make me worry again, love. You've earned yourself a spanking." He winked when she squeaked and slipped around his spouses to relieve Sya'tia of her burden.

Sya'tia smiled at him warmly and allowed him to take one of the wrapped and covered pots she was carrying. "Thank you, Daeshen." She lowered her eyes demurely and followed him into the kitchen. Placing the pan she was carrying onto the counter she began to remove the wrappings while Daeshen bustled about busily behind her, taking out serving dishes and implements.

An arm slipped around her waist, surprising her into dropping the lid she had just taken off with a clatter. She looked behind her and saw Thea peering curiously over her shoulder. Thea hugged her casually, still inspecting the contents of the pan.

"Smells good! What it is?"

"Uhh. It's lovoya in creamstal sauce," she stammered breathlessly.

"Wazzat?" Thea took another appreciative sniff.

"Lovoya is a made from the new tentacles of a creature similar to your octopus and creamstal is the powered shell of a snail on our home."

Thea watched as the other woman stirred the concoction, and felt herself turn faintly green with nausea. Thea swallowed hard. "Sounds lovely." She made a strategic retreat lest she insult her new friend. She heard Daeshen exclaim in excitement and turned to see him stick a finger in the mixture. He licked it off with a blissful expression.

Sya'tia blushed with pleasure over his reaction. "It's my family's recipe."

He laid a smacking kiss on her cheek. "It's wonderful; I can't wait to eat it!"

She giggled and pushed him away.

Thea turned. Kyrin was watching her thoughtfully. "What?"

He smiled. "How did you like the temple?"

She shrugged, walking slowly toward him, trailing her fingers along the edge of the table. "I like Kyaness. She explained quite a bit to me. She asked me to come back again. I think I will." Reaching him, she placed her hand on his chest. "I'm sorry I got mad. This is all so overwhelming for me. Every time I think I'm getting a handle on something another surprise pops up and knocks me on my ass."

Kyrin covered her hand with his. He smiled suddenly and knelt before her, still holding her hand to him. "Theadora, in the eyes of my people we are already mated. But, would you consent to a formal marriage ceremony and accept myself and Daeshen as your husbands in the eyes of your people?" He reached into his pocket with his free hand and withdrew a small object. He slowly held his hand up to her and opened his fingers. A small ring of silvery blue metal rested in his palm.

Thea gasped softly, touching it with just the tips of her fingers. The metal was etched. Small Ta'e'shian figures swam and embraced along its smooth surface. "It's beautiful." She smiled down at him, charmed by his proposal, and touched by his attempt to show her that he respected her and her culture. "Yes, I will marry you in the eyes of my people and by the rituals of my God and Goddess." She held out her hand so that he could slip the ring onto her finger. It was a perfect fit.

Kyrin stood and kissed her gently, coaxing her mouth open under his so that his tongue could make gentle forays inside. He cradled her against his hard frame.

* * *

Corvin frowned at the data he had received from Sara's cerebcom. "This can't be right."

Reba looked up from where she was writing a report and making notes on her holoreader. They were sharing Corvin's office until the new offices for the human medical staff could be completed. "What can't be right?"

Corvin's hair twisted against the front of his jacket in agitation. "According to these readings the seizure never took place. It also hasn't been tracking her hormonal changes like it was supposed to..." His voice trailed off as he began to look for other anomalies.

The cerebral computers were implanted below the left earlobe; they linked the crew's brains directly to the ship computer. This allowed information to be fed directly to them. It also allowed them to communicate directly with one another, without having to use the telepathy inherent to their race.

They also monitored vital statistics and could be used to control the chemical and hormone releases in both races. All humans were given subliminal messages to calm them anytime the cerebcom registered a negative emotional spike.

* * *

Thea eyed the gray tentacle dangling from the tines of her fork dubiously. A white drop of goo oozed. It dripped onto her plate. She slid Sya'tia a sideways look. The other woman beamed proudly as she waited with an expectant expression.

The men didn't disappoint her either. They both took bites and moaned like it was the best sex they had ever had in their lives. Thea braced herself and took a bite, trying very hard not to think of what she was putting in her mouth. She had visions of Japanese anime tentacle critters writhing in black pools of water.

She chewed gingerly. It had the texture of undercooked pasta and tasted a bit like pork. The *creamstal* sauce reminded her of toasted almonds and wasabi, not flavors she would normally put together, but they were very good. She chewed with more enthusiasm. After swallowing she paused for a moment to contemplate this new taste. "I like this." She smiled shyly at Sya'tia, who glowed in response.

Kyrin asked Daeshen a question and the resulting answer had all of them enjoying a lively conversation through the rest of dinner and well into the clean up.

Once the last dish was cleaned and put away they retired to the living room with a plate of crispy treats that the woman had stopped by the galley to acquire since Thea had not had time to make them. Thea marveled again at the food preparation units. *Just like something outta Star Trek! I wonder why so many people cook when they have those.*

They all settled in to watch the movie Thea had picked out. Sya'tia asked a few questions about the novel she was reading while the opening credits rolled.

Daeshen got up and disappeared briefly. He returned with a tray of drinks, a carbonated fruit juice that Thea was quickly becoming partial to. After passing them out he lay down with his head in Thea's lap to watch the movie.

She absently stroked his hair as the first scene started. The room became very quiet as the dialogue began.

* * *

Reba stretched. "I'm heading out, Dr. C; I need food and a hug. See you tomorrow afternoon? Are we pulling Holly out of stasis or not?"

Corvin rubbed his eyes tiredly. "Not yet. I think we should concentrate on Sara and Elaine right now. I also want to go over the other cerebcom records before we bring another woman out of it. Have the other ladies finished working with the asana yet? I think we are going to need their counseling skills more than I first thought."

"I'll check before I come in tomorrow." She paused at the door and smiled at him. "Thank you for helping us find a place here, Dr. C, all the women appreciate it. I'm just sorry my training is something that we need." She waved and the door hissed shut behind her.

Corvin looked down at the figures on his holoreader. "So am I."

He dropped his stylus on the reader and stretched slowly against the back of his chair, closing his eyes when he felt several vertebras pop back into place. He twisted gently from side to side before relaxing again. Picking up several items he began to clean his desk in preparation of leaving his office for the evening.

He paused as his attention was caught by the information being displayed on his holoreader. Apparently he had accessed a hidden file when he had dropped his stylus. Picking it up, he read several programming notations. Each notation seemed to cause the cerebcom to react to images, thought patterns or questions asked of the victim. Should one of the parameters be activated it could cause the cerebcom to vibrate against the bone it rested against. The result would cause heat to generate and nausea from the vibrations so close to the inner ear.

He quickly dug out another holoreader and requested the reports on human physiology. *Hmm... The heat would cause the seizures. Now... Can we reverse it? I should be able to reprogram the com...* He scribbled notes on yet another holoreader.

* * *

Thea looked down at her snoring husband. She poked him in the side. He snorted and rolled over, making soft smacking sounds with his mouth. His nose nuzzled her stomach.

She grinned at Sya'tia, who grinned back.

A moment later he started drooling.

* * *

Corvin smiled smugly as he leaned back in his chair. "This will work." He sent several commands to the women's cerebcoms. As far as he could tell from his calculations this new set of commands should counter the programming previously entered. As an added precaution he added a little trap in case someone should try to reset the programming.

That completed he set instructions to have every other humans cerebcoms tested for the hidden commands. He cracked his knuckles. If the program worked the way he hoped it would a list of all the other women who had been targeted would be downloaded into his holoreader.

He made a few more notes indicating that the list of women that should be revealed would be used as evidence when the attacker was apprehended. He had been researching some of the laws in the United States, where most of the women on their ship had been taken from, and found several mentions of something called "stalking." Perhaps that information should be given to the asana. They might want to use it in the trial, since it was clearly something that was happening here and it was not something that the Ta'e'sha had ever dealt with before.

* * *

Thea poked Daeshen in the side.

He grunted and swatted at her hand.

She grinned and scraped her fingernails down his spine.

He shivered and rolled onto his stomach, wiggling his mouth into the juncture of her thighs.

She blushed when Sya'tia giggled softly.

Sya'tia smirked as she watched Daeshen's hand creep toward Thea's side.

Thea suddenly screamed and bucked as Daeshen's nimble fingers flew up and down her side. Her hands swatted franticly as she tried to push him off her lap and catch his tickling fingers at the same time. Elbows flew, making Kyrin and Sya'tia duck and dive out of the way.

Kyrin laughed and dove back in, attacking Daeshen from behind. He grabbed his husband's foot and scraped his nails along the sole.

Daeshen screeched and bucked on Thea.

Thea's breath left her in a whoosh as Daeshen's head banged into her stomach as he flipped over onto his side. She glared at Sya'tia, who was sitting clear of the flailing limbs and laughing like a loon. Wiggling, she managed to get out from under Daeshen and pounced on her friend and pulled her into the fray as well.

Sya'tia laughed and held Daeshen down so that Thea and Kyrin could tickle him without a shred of mercy.

Several minutes later the Triumphant Trio crowed happily as they eyed their vanquished foe. He lay curled in a fetal position, laughing till tears leaked out his eyes.

Kyrin levered himself up and grinned down at the red juice soaking the front of his clothes. "Who spilled the drink?"

Sya'tia grinned and slung her arm around Thea's shoulders. "I think it was an unnamed foot." She snickered. "I might be able to identify it in a line up, though. But a proper application of fingernails would be needed to make a positive identification."

Both men scooted away hurriedly.

Daeshen leaned back and grinned at the two lovely ladies curled together on the dry side of the bowl. "Thea, would you like to go with me to the pool tomorrow? I'm meeting my team there so we can go over the lists the Lithen gave us."

"Okay, sounds fun."

Kyrin disappeared into the other room to get a towel to clean up the spilled juice. "We might also need your help, love. We want to set up a few spaces for shops and restaurants, and we thought we would use some of the human styles," he called back.

Thea looked at Daeshen. He shrugged.

"We thought the ladies would like some familiar surroundings."

She smiled slowly. "That's a good idea. You should ask Shana to help you with the restaurants. A beauty salon would be nice, too. I'd like to check out some of the shops here on the ship soon, too."

Sya'tia eyed her curiously. "Tell me about beauty salons."

Thea slipped her arm around her waist and the women began discussing the merits of a beauty salon.

Chapter Twelve

Barik took a deep drink from the glass in front of him and watched the human females laugh and talk to his people. His upper lip twitched slightly. *Filthy things. Ugly. Inferior. Disgusting. How can my people think they are our hope? How can men mate with them? Touch them? And like it.* His skin crawled. He did what he had to do, not because he actually liked having to touch those disgusting creatures.

A faint smirk pulled the corners of his lips as he thought about the last female, he couldn't even think of them as women, he had punished. By the time he had finished with her he had degraded her to the point that she was the grunting, whining animal he knew her to be. He'd laughed and taunted her, as she lay tied to the bed and helpless in the empty cabin he liked to use.

Then he spent several minutes slowly plucking strands of fur from her mound. Finishing that, he had rubbed his semen into her skin "You'll never be rid of me. I will permeate your skin forever," he'd murmured against her ear.

His thoughts turned to his sister. Darling, beloved, child sister. Balai had been the only daughter born of his five parents. His branch of the clan had never been one to bear many daughters, and so Balai was to join the clan council when she came of age. Her first husband would have joined her on the council, helping her make decisions for them all. Sweet tempered and joyful, she had been loved by the whole family and much of the small town their parents called home.

The royal clans of the Ta'e'sha were matriarchal. The power to rule was passed from daughter to daughter, assuring that the bloodline continued, since there had been no way to prove who fathered the children centuries ago.

His fingers tightened around the glass in his hand, threatening to crush it. She had barely survived the virus, only to find that she could not bear children. *She loved children. She always spent her free time in the nurseries.*

In the end she could not bear it. A few sips of poisoned wine and she was gone.

Only afterwards did he discover that the women already on the council had preserved their own eggs. As a precaution against the loss of their line through assassination or illness. His mother was past childbearing age and since Balai had not taken her seat on the council her eggs had not been harvested. His sister could have used one of their mother's remaining eggs to have children, but she killed herself before she knew that it was a possibility.

Then those bastards decided to replace our women. "Oh, we are distraught! The tragedy of it all. Gee, guess we'll just find someone else to breed on. Go find some animals while we impregnate ourselves with our own eggs." Yes, they were so sympathetic... As if our beautiful women were nothing to them. After all, their own lines were secure. He ground his teeth as he watched the little red haired woman who he would punish next. *Intelligent animals, barbarians. Ungrateful beasts... Whining about being taken, as if their dirt grubbing lives were so much better before. But those who are happy... Oh, they know. That makes them even worse. I'm sure they secretly laugh at our childless women. Feeling so superior as our men rut on them.*

He was distracted from his thoughts by Daeshen coming in with his arm wrapped around his tiny mate. She confused him. She seemed to accept her mates and everyone else, but at the same time she seemed distant from it all. It was as if she were watching from the other side of a window. It made him uneasy. Those eyes of hers watching him, as if she could see his soul.

As he watched, Theadora hugged one of the security officers taking her lunch. A slight shimmer on her cheeks drew his eye. He set down his glass and moved to a position for a better view. *What is that?* Her hands waved as she talked animatedly with the other woman. Light blue-green markings covered the backs of her hands and wrists. *Are those...? No, they can't be...*

They were.

He felt his blood burn in his veins. His vision blurred and darkened. Barik looked down quickly, forcing himself to calm so that his hunting lenses receded. He drew in several slow deep breaths. *Even the Gods forsake our women.* He looked back up and watched her. *I'll take her... And let it be spit in Their faces. How dare They abandon us as well?*

Chapter Thirteen

"Wow." Thea stared upwards at the blazing artificial sun. The Ta'e'sha had recreated a forest and lake from their home, complete with a perfectly detailed sky. She looked around, mouth open. Trees grew straight and tall on gently rolling hills. Yellow-green grass was lush and thick under her feet. Wildly colored flowers sprouted in beautiful, random bunches. "It's beautiful." And it was at least the size of a football field.

Daeshen grinned and tugged her toward the lake in the center of the room. It sat there gleaming like a blue jewel. Several small islands rose from the center, covered with a thick layer of black-green moss and small, smooth barked saplings

Several people swam and sunned themselves on the bank. It was like a scene from a faerie tale. Scales and fins flashed and sparkled everywhere she looked.

"Uh, Daeshen? Are those two doing what I think they are?"

He looked in the direction Thea was and smiled. He took her hand and towed her to the edge of the lake and began taking his clothes off. "Yup, they are. Want to watch?"

Her cheeks burned with sudden color. "No!" She snuck another quick glance at the couple making passionate love in the water.

He quickly stripped and slid into the water. A moment later his legs joined, forming a deep blue tail the color of his eyes.

Thea sat down on the edge and tried to ignore the naked people strolling around. Several people swam toward them, calling out to Daeshen.

He greeted them and introduced Thea. They were members of his science team. The conversation quickly turned technical. The group had originally planned to discuss the flora and fauna on the lists, but were sidetracked by some new data they had heard about from one of the other teams. Apparently, a man had eaten a slice of key lime pie his mate had made and it had an *uplifting* effect on him that had taken hours to subside. The other team had decided to run a few tests...

Thea's eyes crossed as she listened to the group discuss the chemical reaction that caused it, although, she thought Daeshen was cute when he geeked out. Losing interest, she looked around curiously, absently listening to the gabble. A short, pink haired woman approached the water a few feet away from them and, without a shred of modesty, whipped off her robe and dove into the water.

A moment later she surfaced and lolled onto her back, floating lazily in the water. She turned her head and noticed Thea watching her. She smiled and waved. When Thea waved back she rolled over and made her way to where Thea was sitting with strong movements of her tail.

Reaching the side she levered herself out of the water and sat beside Thea. Her deep pink tail dangled in the water. "Hi, I'm Kati. Who are you? I've never seen you here before. Have you been on the ship long? What's it like having hair? Are you pregnant? Who's your mate?" She paused for a breath and beamed at Thea.

Thea blinked.

"Uhh... I'm Thea, I haven't been here long," she paused trying to remember the rest of that string of questions. "Hair can be fun, but pain to style sometimes. Umm... I don't know if I'm pregnant and Kyrin and Daeshen are my mates. Did I miss anything?" Thea tried to ignore the small breasts waving in her face. *This is disconcerting.*

Daeshen turned to see whom she was talking to. "Hello, Kati, how are your parents?" He smiled at the exuberant young woman.

"They're great! My dads aren't really happy about me swimming in the adult pool now, but I'm old enough so they just glower a lot." She grinned mischievously. "I didn't know you were mated! Mom said the captain had, but she didn't say anything about you!" She turned to Thea and said earnestly, "Kyrin and Daeshen are really nice."

Daeshen winked and tweaked the girl's nose before returning to his conversation.

Kati fidgeted a little. "Wanna swim with me? Can you swim? Oh, wow, there's Soren..." The endless string of questions trailed off as she gazed behind Thea longingly. "He's so handsome..."

Thea grinned and turned. Soren was bouncing around in his usual energetic way. Seeing her he waved and promptly tripped. She hid a laugh and motioned him to her when he picked himself up.

He hurried over. Spotting Kati he came to a dead stop, blushed deep red and mumbled a hello.

Good Lord, they're like a couple of lovesick teenagers. She watched them stare at each other, conversation and Thea forgotten. She cleared her throat, making them both jump. "So... Soren, I was hoping to see you at the temple tomorrow."

He sat down, sneaking little glances at Kati, who was suddenly fascinated with the grass she was sitting on. "Oh, um, yeah, sure, I'll be there, Thea. How have you been Kati? Have you finished your classes yet?" He turned to Thea. "Kati is an acid painter, a really good one!"

Kati blushed and stammered a denial.

"What's an acid painter?" Thea asked Kati, tilting her head curiously.

"Umm... Crystals from the crystalshrooms are dropped in acid and then we use a metal stylus to apply the mixture to glass. The acids etch the glass and the crystal that is used in it creates color. You have to be very careful when you do it; the acid is very strong," came the soft reply.

Soren beamed proudly. "She's one of the best! As soon as her classes are finished Kyrin wants to give her a shop to display her wares on the ship." His face fell. "That is, if you stay... Now that you're an adult you can return to Ta'e."

Kati picked at some grass. "I'm staying on the ship. It's home now and there are so many things to see." She peeked up at him. "And there are a few other reasons I want to stay..."

He blushed again. "That's good; I'd miss you if you were gone."

Kati bit her lip. "I'm supposed to move into my own quarters at the end of the week, Soren. Could you help me? I'll make you dinner. You too, Thea," she added hastily.

"I would be happy to help," she replied and listened to the two of them stumble and work their way toward their first date. *Wow, clumsy dating is universal.* It made her feel good and as if she had more in common with the Ta'e'sha than before. A tall man with the same pink hair as Kati strode toward them with a determined expression on his face. *Looks like overprotective daddies are universal, too.* She stood quickly and brushed off her skirt.

She held out her hand as he reached them and rushed to greet him as his mouth opened. "Hi, I'm Theadora Auralel; you must be Kati's father. I can see where she gets her good looks! Soren and Kati were just telling me about acid painting, would you care to join us? They have both been very welcoming to me, and it's been such a pleasure getting to know them."

The thundercloud expression on his face faded to confusion as he stared down at her. He stared at her hand for a moment before tentatively grasping it. He squeezed gently for a moment before releasing. "Hello, Theadora, a pleasure to meet you." He gazed at the markings on her face in confusion. "You are Chosen of our Gods?"

Thea touched her cheek self-consciously. "Sorta. I don't worship them, but they asked to use my voice and when I woke up these were here. I'm more worried my Lord and Lady will be offended. The marks are pretty, though." She was starting to get used to seeing them on her skin. The first few days they had caught her eye every time she moved.

He blinked and stepped back, a look of awe on his face. "I see."

Kati tugged on his arm. "*Deema*, father, Soren and Thea are going to help me move to my new quarters! Isn't that sweet of them?"

He smiled down at his daughter. "That's very nice, dear heart. Be sure you don't make a nuisance of yourself to Mistress Theadora, though."

Thea sat down and smiled up at him, patting the space beside her in invitation. "Oh, she could never be a nuisance! I've been quite enjoying the warmth; it's nice to be around someone so open and friendly. And please call me Thea."

He settled beside her. "I am called Paeten." He nodded at Soren in greeting, who smiled nervously in response. "What line of work are you in, Thea? I work in the science department, with your mate Daeshen." He smiled wryly. "But not in the key lime pie division."

"I'm a weaver." She looked to check where her husband was, catching the smile he sent to her. "Mostly cloth, but I also weave tapestries."

Paeten nodded. "A most respected occupation, I would enjoy seeing your work. I have not had the opportunity to spend much time with the ladies who have joined us." He crossed his legs and watched his daughter talk quietly with Soren.

"You are more than welcome to visit. I'll show you my work room. Daeshen hung several of my pieces in our quarters, so there are plenty to show you." She leaned back on a palm and followed his gaze to his daughter. "It must be hard watching them leave the nest."

He glanced at her. "I beg your pardon? What nest?"

She smiled ruefully. "I mean watching your daughter grow up and move out."

"Ahh, yes it is, and she is the first..." He smiled fondly. "But you cannot keep them children forever. I think it's harder for the fathers when daughters leave. After all, I know what that young man is thinking." He laughed when Soren darted a glance at him, paled and gulped.

After a few more minutes of conversation Paeten excused himself and Soren and Kati drifted off in the water still talking animatedly. Thea had a brief thought of what their kids would be like. Talking nonstop and tripping over everything. Ye Gods.

She watched the groups of people around her, noticing the differences in their builds and appearances. She gasped softly as a woman with pale blue-gray skin and hair swam past her. Her tail was moving from side to side instead of the up and down motion she was accustomed to seeing. The shape of her tail was like a shark. Looking more closely, she noted that the tails of the Ta'e'sha people seemed to be very similar to several different species of fish from her home. *So, maybe they have different races like we do?* She tried to match the shapes of tails to different places on her planet to pass the time while her husband was busy.

Daeshen's team left a bit later and he pulled himself up to sit next to her and began unbuttoning her blouse.

"Hey! What are you doing?" Thea swatted his hands and held the edges of her blouse together.

He smirked and tugged her blouse out of her hands and whipped it off. He attacked the buttons down the side of her skirt next. "I'm taking you to that pretty little spot in the center of the lake and I'm going to fuck that pretty little pussy of yours," he whispered in her ear. Wrapping an arm around her hips he pulled her into the water with him and swam slowly toward the center of the lake, ignoring her grumbles and wiggles as she tried to get loose.

"I am *not* having sex in public!" Her legs slid against his tail and she felt that warm melting in her loins again as he rubbed his chest against her breasts, which were barely covered by her see-through lace bra.

He hummed softly and lazily weaved his way through a group of people caressing each other intimately. "Don't you want to know how we make love in the water? No one would be able to see very much that way, lover. Besides, it's perfectly natural for our people." He licked the shell of her ear slowly, making her shiver. She looked so cute as she glowered at him.

She looked at him and muttered, "That's just mean! You know how curious I am! Can't we go home and use the tub?" She nibbled on his chin enticingly. Her head came up in a rush when she felt hands stroke down her body as they passed a pair of men.

Daeshen winked at the men, both of whom sent very complimentary comments about his wife's pale skin and dark hair. Reaching a spot hidden in a thick ring of reeds Daeshen slowed and lolled on his back. He gently stroked her as she looked around cautiously. Sliding his hand up her back he released the clasp of her bra with a deft twist of his wrist.

She laughed softly, relaxing against him. The reeds provided a semblance of privacy. She looped her arms around his neck as his hands slipped into her panties to caress her bottom. Sitting up, she straddled his lap and slid her bra off her arms and tossed it behind her.

Several catcalls were yelled out beyond the reeds a moment later along with a few offers that made her blush.

He laughed softly. "We are a bit freer about sex than your culture." He leaned up and licked the soft skin between her breasts. "We occasionally take lovers if our mates don't mind. I think a few of those men are hoping you'll ask them to join us." He caught a nipple in his lips and suckled gently, enjoying the way her back arched in response. His fingers slid into the sides of her panties and he quickly tore the seams. He slowly tugged them from between her legs.

Thea moaned as the lace slid between the lips of her pussy and rasped against her clit. After several delicious moments it came free.

Daeshen threw it over her shoulder, setting off another round of catcalls.

She giggled and hid her face in his shoulder. "I don't think I'm ready for another one of you perverts yet." She nipped his nose, making him laugh.

He stroked her breasts again and pushed her up. Taking her hand in his he stroked her palm down his chest and over his abdomen.

She slipped her hand free to explore his body. Her fingers slid over where his skin formed in scales. Tiny scales flickered in the sunlight. He was smooth and firm under her fingertips. His tail felt like a solid column of muscle. The scales were as smooth as glass. She stroked lower, brushing her palms back and forth over his hips. It was just so amazing to her that they could change shape!

A slit opened over his groin and his penis slowly emerged. Heavy and hard it lay against his belly and throbbed.

She grasped it firmly and stroked slowly up and down. With her free hand she tickled the opening in his body, making him squirm under her and the water lap along her hips. She smiled and placed her hands on his chest and rubbed herself along his heated length.

He growled softly and pulled her down into his arms and took her mouth hard, devouring her sweetness. His fingers tested her wetness and he moaned into her mouth when he found her already moist and hot for him. "Gods, you are perfect, darling," he breathed against her lips.

He helped her raise herself above him and moaned as she sank slowly down upon him. He urged her hips into a slow up and down grind that he matched with slow undulations of his body. His hands slid up to cup her breasts and rubbed them with gentle circular motions.

Thea held his wrists as she rocked and ground down on him. She barely lifted herself off him before sliding back down; the sensation of fullness was incredible. Her head fell back, letting her hair trail in the water lapping over her husband's tail. Releasing his hands she leaned back, placing her palms on his tail behind her and began to work her hips in circles. The sensation was incredible, she felt so full and his trembling frills rasped along the walls of her moist sheath delightfully.

Daeshen's breath hissed out from behind his clenched teeth. "Oh yeah... Just like that... Harder now." He twisted her nipples, making her jerk on him. He moaned in response.

She came to a stop and smiled evilly down at him, causing his eyebrows to arch. Her sheath contracted slowly around him. She held her muscles taut for a moment then released them. Her fingers slid between their bodies and she stroked the sensitive opening in his tail. Contracting again, she smirked as he started to thrash under her and mumble hot, sexy words.

He shouted and grabbed her, yanking her down onto his chest. Fixing his hands on her bottom he began thrusting frenziedly into her. He growled when she bit his neck and screamed. Two more thrusts and he felt her tighten and ripple around him. He let himself go and with a final thrust lodged himself deep and began pulsing his cream into her.

She panted and rested against him for a moment. Sex with Kyrin and Daeshen always blew her mind. They found her limits and pushed, driving her to new heights every time. And yet, she always felt their affection and care. She sat up and let her head fall back as she breathed slowly. "Mmm..." She stroked his chest in slow, lazy motions as she savored the last shocks of her orgasm.

He caressed her hips, admiring her body. Twisting deftly, he levered them upright in the water and kissed her lazily. Lips gently stroking against each other as the last pulses left his body. Lifting his head he smiled wickedly. "How do you like the lake, darling?"

She giggled softly, hiding her face in his neck. "I like it, brat."

* * *

Two weeks later...

Thea frowned at the swirling letters in the oversized book in her hand. She rubbed her eyes tiredly. *This stuff is hard on the eyes.* "Soren, are you sure this book isn't in the computer so I can read it in English?"

Soren looked up from his own text with glazed eyes. They cleared after a moment. "No, besides you should practice our script anyway, you never know when you might need it."

She sighed and went back to reading. It was a book on Ta'e'shian marriage customs. "According to this you offer a scarf made in the same colors as the woman you are offering marriage to. Right?"

He nodded and set aside the religious text he had been studying. "That's right. If she accepts the scarf it means she accepts your suit."

"Okay, so it's like offering an engagement ring."

"I guess so." He tapped the ring on her finger. "Is that an engagement ring?"

She nodded, not looking up. "Kyrin studied our customs and had it made for me. Wasn't that sweet of him?" She paused in her reading and admired her ring again.

"Uh, yes. But, aren't you already mated?"

"Yes, by Ta'e'sha custom, but he wants us to be married by the customs of my religion as well."

"Oh." He frowned. "So, why are you studying our customs?"

A bit of color flushed warmly into her cheeks. "Oh, just curious..." she said evasively and neatly turned the conversation to another subject. "I wish there was someplace where we could make small temples and chapels. I'd imagine the other women would like some place to pray."

Soren was quickly distracted by the mention of other religions, and started asking questions as fast as Kati.

* * *

Corvin stepped into Kyrin's office, tapping a holoreader against his leg. "We have enough evidence to arrest Barik, Captain." He set the reader in front of his captain and sat down heavily. "We have the testimony of the two women out of stasis, proof of his tampering with their cerebcoms, physical evidence from his sperm on their skin, and extreme vaginal ripping. He withdrew before his frills folded."

Kyrin winced and turned gray. The spines in their frills would have lanced the women's vaginas and torn the length down. "What else?"

The doctor rubbed his face; he looked haggard and haunted from his experiences of the last few days. "We will continue to revive the remaining women and interview them. Some will need surgery. The women mentioned specific tortures and verbal abuse. He was brutal, thorough and clinical. Elaine said she would have been able to accept the rape better if he hadn't been so cold and calculating. She said it was like she wasn't even important and just seemed to be someone he picked randomly, which we know is not the case."

Kyrin scanned the information on the holoreader and swallowed repeatedly. "I'll have the security officers arrest him and place him in the brig. I think it's best if he were placed in stasis until we get home and have the trial there." He tapped a few keys on the holoreader to approve the order and sent it to security.

A confirmation code of the arrest order logging itself in the ship's computer and in his personal logs flashed on the screen a moment later. Security confirmed that they received the order and were currently attempting to locate the subject. They would contact him upon the subject's arrest.

Kyrin leaned over his desk and placed a hand on his friend's shoulder. "Go home, Corvin, give yourself some time, you don't have to do it all at once." He squeezed Corvin's shoulder gently. "He'll be in custody in a few minutes. You won't do the women any good if you drop from exhaustion or become numb to what's happened to them."

The other man nodded and rose from his chair. "I know, Kyrin, I just wish we could have prevented this. What he did... How could I work with him everyday and not see that something was wrong?"

"No one knew, Corvin. How could we?" Kyrin escorted him to the door. "It's not your fault."

* * *

Thea hummed softly to herself as she walked toward home. Her hand rubbed across her belly. She had felt queasy this morning when she woke up. *I think I'll ask Corvin to give me a pregnancy test tomorrow before I go to the temple.*

She smiled to herself; her husbands were going to be ecstatic. She was actually excited about the thought of being pregnant.

Spending time at the Ta'e'shian temples had made her feel closer to her own Lord and Lady. Thea had always held the belief that you didn't need a special place to be with your God or Gods because nothing was as sacred as holding them in one's heart. And, as a direct result her mind calmed when she was there and she was able to work her way through the many things that had been happening to her. She was able to step back and look at Daeshen and Kyrin and actually see them. It was very easy to like what she saw, too.

In fact, as she learned more of the Ta'e'shian culture the more she liked it. Equality between the sexes was such an established belief that it never crossed their minds to treat men, or women, differently. It was very interesting to her that there were no insults in their society based on sexuality. To them, sex was a very natural thing and not something to be mocked or ashamed of. She pondered the interesting fact she had learned from Kyaness today.

Prostitution had no negative connotations in their society; it was considered a necessary service, performed by trained professionals. It was actually very common for parents to take their children to such a professional when they reached adulthood, ensuring that the loss of their virginity was pleasant and done with care. This was especially important to the young men, Kyaness had explained to her. Their frills could cause internal damage if they tried to withdraw too soon.

She turned down a corridor. It had become her habit to walk the living sections corridors home because there were fewer people in them to bother her. It gave her time to absorb what she had studied that day and think of new questions she wanted to ask.

She was absently aware of the hiss of a door opening behind her. She smacked her neck when she felt a faint sting on it, catching a hand. Her legs gave out when she tried to turn as a strange tingle sped through her limbs, leaving a burning, aching paralysis behind.

Barik's face leaned over her. His lips stretched in a macabre smirk as he quickly picked her up and carried her into the cabin she had passed moments before.

Chapter Fourteen

"Captain, we are unable to locate the subject. His cerebcom is not responding to our queries. We will begin a search of the ship immediately."

Kyrin frowned and rubbed his forehead. It had just begun aching, along with a general ache all over his body. The message that he had just received didn't help. "Very well, keep me updated on your progress. And find out why his cereb is not responding! That shouldn't be possible!"

* * *

Daeshen rubbed his shoulder. *Ow, am I coming down with something?* His legs and chest began to ache as well. His stomach lurched evilly for a moment and then steadied. Sweat broke out across his brow.

* * *

The top of Sya'tia's neck tightened and throbbed. She looked around predatorily. That sensation always preceded something bad happening.

After several minutes of nothing to explain the sensation she rolled her shoulders and neck to loosen the muscles and continued questioning people as to whether they had seen Barik.

* * *

Thea screamed in her head. Not a single muscle responded when she tried to move and it felt like she was burning from the inside. Terror rose inside her like a tsunami.

Barik dropped her carelessly on the floor and stalked around her, inspecting her. Suddenly he knelt down and grabbed a hank of her hair and pulled her head up. He traced a nail along the markings on her cheek. "Chosen by the Lithen..."

Her cheek exploded in pain as he suddenly, viciously, slapped her. Her head landed on the floor with a thump when he let her hair go. She saw his leg cock back and whimpered.

He landed a vicious kick to her midsection. The force slid her several feet across the floor.

Agony burst in her abdomen, but all she could do was pant. *My baby! Please Lady, Lord! Help me!* Wetness seeped between her legs and began to soak into the dark fabric of her pants. *Nononono! Please, no!* She watched as he approached her, lifted his foot and kicked her again, across her chest. Her breath whooshed out, and in her paralyzed state she was unable to regain it. Her mind scrabbled furiously, like a terrified animal.

Barik snarled his hand in her hair and dragged her dead weight across the floor and into the next room. "They won't want you when I'm done, your mates will turn from you in

disgust and you'll never want to show your face ever again."
Dropping her again he knelt and stroked her cheek gently.
"This isn't about you, female. It's restitution. Justice for our
women and my sister." He brushed her hair from her face.
"They don't care about them anymore, you see…"

Black dots swam before Thea's eyes. Her breath was
starting to come back to her slowly. A deep, tearing cramp
clenched her abdomen. Tears trickled from her eyes. *Please
stop, please stop… I never hurt you… My baby…*

He drew a knife from inside his uniform and pressed the
blade against her cheek. "Does the venom hurt? Does it
burn? I asked the other women, but, of course, they couldn't
answer. I hope it does." He slid the knife inside her shirt and
cut it open with a quick jerk. "You were so nice… Except
those eyes…" he crooned softly. "Could you see into my soul,
Theadora? That's how it felt. I'm going to cut them out, you
know, those too seeing eyes." He tossed the knife aside and
tore the shirt from her body.

"But not yet. You have to see what I do to you. You have
to hurt more. Take the pain. Share it with our faithless Gods.
Let them look on your scarred and blind face." Balling his
fists he began to slowly and methodically beat her.

She couldn't move. She couldn't fight back. All Thea
could do was accept the pain and feel her child's life stream
from her body in a trickle of blood.

* * *

Kyrin dove into restroom just off his office and retched
violently into the toilet. He wiped his mouth with a
trembling hand. Standing on shaking legs he stumbled to the

door. "Whist, help me get to sick bay." He sagged against the jamb as the younger man ran to him. Another tearing cramp in his belly doubled him over.

Whist wrapped his arm around his captain's waist and helped him to the elevator. "What's wrong?" He waved away several other members of the crew who rushed over to help, and punched the button for the correct floor.

Kyrin shook his head. "I don't know, my muscles started aching and cramping and I just threw up. Gods, I feel awful, I hope Daeshen and Thea haven't caught it, whatever it is."

The door opened and Whist half carried Kyrin down the hall to the sick bay. On the way he commed Daeshen. "*Are you all right? The captain is very ill; I'm taking him to sick bay.*"

"*Send someone for me, Whist,*" came the weak reply. "*I don't think I can make it on my own.*"

"*Will do. Is Thea sick as well?*"

"*I don't know, she's still at the Balance Temple with Soren.*"

* * *

Barik took out a small scalpel and smiled down at Thea's terrified, blood-streaked face.

* * *

Corvin entered medical and took in the scene with a glance. "Status." Two nurses were holding Daeshen and Kyrin as they vomited repeatedly into containers.

The doctor in charge handed him a holoreader. "No sign of disease or poisoning. They both claim muscle aches and cramping, then soon after began vomiting."

He nodded, scanning the information on the reader. "Is their mate sick as well?"

"No one has brought her in or reported it."

Corvin frowned. If two were sick there was a good chance all three were. "Daeshen, where's Thea?"

Daeshen rested the side of his face against the container and panted. "She's at the temple with Soren."

Corvin quickly commed Soren, *"Soren, is Thea sick? Both Kyrin and Daeshen are very ill."*

"I don't know, she left over half an hour ago, Chief Medic," came the worried reply. *"She was fine when she left."*

He immediately commed security, *"Please locate Theadora Auralel, possible medical emergency. She is human and doesn't not know how to use her com fully yet. She has been missing at least thirty minutes and if ill may be incapacitated."*

"Searching," was the succinct reply.

A moment passed.

"She has been located; a security team is already nearby and will reach her location in approximately two minutes." There was a pause. *"Why would she be in an unoccupied cabin?"*

* * *

Thea screamed in her head again. Agony flared along every inch of her body. Her eyes were swollen almost completely shut from the beating and blood streamed from several shallow cuts he'd made on her face before he had begun cutting along the marks on her chest. *Lord and Lady, bear witness through my eyes.* A curious numbness spread through her body, distancing her from the pain.

Barik frowned as the female's muscles twitched under his scalpel as he carefully cut around the God-markings on her chest. "Oh dear, they won't be clear lines." He casually slapped her face. "Be still."

He finished the cut and edged the knife under her skin and carefully cut it from the muscle underneath. He would cut the marking free of her unworthy flesh. He heard the door open and looked up, angry at being disturbed.

Three security officers stood in the threshold, faces blank with shock. They quickly shook it off and dove for him.

He screamed in rage as the scalpel was wrestled free of his hand and the weight of their bodies carried him to the floor.

They quickly flipped him on his stomach and bound his wrists and feet.

Turning his head he glared at his victim, who stared blankly back at him. Working his mouth he spit on her.

One of the officers took off his shirt and covered Thea's twitching body. He quickly sent a brief report and requested additional officers. He picked her up carefully, "I'll take her to sick bay; stay here with him and report to me as soon as he's in the brig." With that he left in a smooth jog, trying to be careful not to jar the woman in his arms. As he moved swiftly through the maze of corridors he commed medical and apprised them of the situation so they would be prepared when he arrived.

Chapter Fifteen

Corvin was in his office when the com came in. He blanched at the brief report of Thea's injuries. He quickly commed the Healing temple and requested two asana join him. That done, he left his office and instructed the nurses to move Kyrin and Daeshen to a private room.

He knew they would be furious, but he couldn't risk having them in the room when Thea came in. And if he told them, they wouldn't leave. Following his nurse, he grabbed a sedative.

"I'm going to put you both to sleep until I know exactly what's happening," he informed them as his nurses settled them on beds.

Kyrin nodded tiredly.

The doctor quickly administered the doses and a moment later both men were asleep.

Just in time, too. From the flurry of activity outside the room the asana had arrived. Corvin didn't want to explain why he'd called them. He went back into the main room.

"What is it, Corvin?" asked Wehtai, the high priestess of the Healing Temple.

"The captain's mate is going to be here in a moment or so, please follow me." He led them into surgery, along with three of his nurses. "Thea has been beaten and tortured, I do not know the full extent of the damage yet, but I asked you to come here as a precaution."

The door burst open as Wehtai opened her mouth to ask more questions.

The security officer quickly set down his burden and backed away. "I got her here as soon as I could. She doesn't respond to anything and hasn't moved a muscle." He backed out the door, leaving the doctors to their work.

Corvin leaned over Thea's still form. He brushed her hair back and checked her eyes. They were dilated and blank with shock. He ignored the gasps from his nurses as they removed the shirt covering her. Straightening, he motioned them back.

Wehtai stepped forward. "Let me, Doctor, you are too close a friend to do this." She took Thea's hand in hers and immediately stiffened into a trance. Her eyes closed and she began reciting a list of injuries in a monotone.

The second asana stepped forward and took Thea's other hand. A warm green glow flowed from their hands and slowly coated Thea.

Minutes passed.

Wehtai looked up without releasing Thea's hand, tears in her eyes. "She's miscarrying her child. We need a Warrior Chosen, Doctor; she was injected with their venom and it's slowing our ability to heal her. I don't think we can save her baby."

The light surrounding Thea intensified as the asana began to heal her injuries. The cuts sealed themselves; the blood slowed and finally stopped. Angry red scars formed and slowly faded to silvery lines.

Thea's eyes flickered and tears began to roll from the corners. *My baby is dead.* She felt the last strand break, and with it, her heart. It was too much. She looked for that numbness that had filled her earlier and sank into its quiet coldness.

*   *   *

Several hours later...

Corvin washed his hands tiredly, fighting back tears. *I should have ordered the arrest sooner.* There were so many things he should have done differently. He had thought that having security watching the women with tampered coms would be enough. Thea was paying for his mistake.

A hand touched his shoulder gently.

He turned to face Wehtai. "This shouldn't have happened," he whispered brokenly.

A door opened behind them and Kyrin stepped out, still pale. Daeshen followed a pace behind. They both stopped when they saw Corvin.

"What's wrong?" Kyrin asked tensely.

"Barik attacked Thea," Corvin whispered.

"Where is she?" Kyrin asked hoarsely.

Both men ran for the room Wehtai pointed at. They came to a stumbling halt when they saw their mate lying under a blanket.

She was staring blankly at the ceiling, tears flowing from her eyes as she blinked slowly. Fading bruises still marked her face.

They hesitantly approached her, and gently took her hands in theirs.

"What did he do to her?" Daeshen asked brokenly.

Corvin stepped into the room and quietly closed the door. "He injected her with the venom of a Warrior. We keep some on hand for each Warrior in case they empty their sacs and cannot replenish it. Then he took her to an empty cabin and beat her. He cut her several times with a scalpel and was trying to cut off her God-marks when security found them. If you hadn't gotten sick…we can't get her to respond to us at all. She…she miscarried a child." He looked down at the fragile figure on the bed, so unlike her usual self.

Daeshen pressed a kiss against her hand. "I think she's empathic. Maybe that's why we got sick, she was asking for help and didn't know how." He pressed his head against her hand again and cried. "Our baby…"

Kyrin stroked his mate's cheek gently, noting every silvery scar. "Corvin, could you leave us alone for awhile?" He was barely aware of his friend nodding and leaving silently. "Come back to us, love. We need you here with us." He pressed her palm against his cheek. "Please, baby…"

Her eyes flickered.

Both men talked to her quietly, urging her to come back, telling her they loved her. She was dimly aware of them, but she was safe where she had locked herself away and was reluctant to return. She knew the pain was waiting to rush in like water the moment she cracked open the numbing cocoon she was in.

An hour passed and her husbands stayed with her. They pulled chairs close to her bed and held her hands. They didn't know what else to do.

Daeshen crawled into Kyrin's lap after a while and they both cried, for the loss of their child, for not being able to stop this from happening, for Thea's pain.

Thea heard weeping and the sound drew her out of her cold shell. She slowly worked her way out of the comforting layers she had built around herself. As her mind rose to consciousness again she felt the ache in her body and the hollow void in her womb. It almost sent her back, but the weeping called to her.

The men didn't notice when her head slowly turned toward them. She reached out a trembling hand and touched Kyrin. "Don't cry," she whispered past sore lips. "It's not your fault."

Daeshen lunged for her, scooped her up, and held her close. He carried her back to Kyrin and they both held her, pressing soft kisses across her face.

She began to cry softly, curling herself tightly against Kyrin's chest. "I couldn't stop him! I tried and tried and I couldn't move." She sobbed harder. "He hit me and kicked me. He killed our baby and I couldn't stop him. And he kept saying he was going to cut out my eyes." Her body shook with the force of her sobs and reliving the terror she had lived through.

Kyrin closed his eyes tightly as he listened to her. He was torn between sorrow and hate. He wanted to kill Barik, slowly and painfully. Instead, he curled his arms around both his mates and rocked them gently, not speaking as Thea continued to tell them what happened to her in a soft, tear choked voice. He kissed the top of Daeshen's head and then Thea's.

The door chimed softly, announcing a visitor.

Daeshen looked up and his eyes darkened. "Who is it?'

"Sya'tia."

Thea didn't raise her head from under Kyrin's chin. "Come in."

The door slid open and Sya'tia entered tentatively. She took a few steps in and stopped, unsure of her welcome.

Thea reached out her hand. "It's all right, come closer." She shuddered as another cramp tightened in her belly. "I could use another hug."

Sya'tia knelt beside them and gave her friend a shaky smile. "You are the one who was hurt, yet you try to comfort us?" She stroked Thea's hair gently.

Thea wiped her eyes. She curled her arm around Sya'tia and hugged her. "Having the three of you here helps." She released the other woman, but laced their fingers together. With a sigh she rested against her husband again. "What will happen to him?"

Kyrin held her tighter. "He'll be placed in stasis and we'll take him back to Ta'e for trial."

She smiled bitterly. "He rapes women, attacks me, kills our child...and gets to take a nap before his trial." She glared down at her lap. "Will it be an impartial trial? After all, it was humans he attacked." She looked up again. "I'm sorry, that wasn't fair."

Sya'tia shook her head. "It's all right, Thea."

The three of them hugged her gently, quietly lending their strength.

Chapter Sixteen

Thea was dimly aware that she was sleeping as she looked around the heavily forested area of her dream. Birds sang softly to each other and flitted from branch to branch. A squirrel scampered through the dry leaves on the ground. Warm golden light laced the leaves over her head and dust danced lightly within them.

She took a deep breath of the oxygen heavy air. It filled her lungs and left in a warm rush. The rich scent of loam and flowers teased her nose. She pressed her palm against the warm bark of a tree and felt it respond with joy and love.

Something buzzed past her ear. Turning her head she watched a dragonfly dart back up into the branches. Somewhere close by a stream babbled gently over age smoothed stones. This place felt like home.

The quiet, natural sounds of life sank into her pores and soothed the rough edges of her emotions.

Trailing her fingers from tree to tree, pausing every so often to stroke the velvety petals of a flower, she meandered her way along the trail she found herself on. Animal faces peered at her from the foliage. A wolf here, a rabbit there. Huge ferns grew with wild abandon beneath the heavy canopy of trees. Their dark green fronds lush and shiny with health.

She came to a circle of massive oaks. They were so large that when she tried to circle one her arms barely curved. A breeze made the leaves chuckle merrily, as if laughing at her like an indulgent uncle.

Thea stepped around one of the trees and stopped. In the center of the circle thirteen stones stood like timeworn sentinels. And within them, two figures waited for her.

There was a woman dressed in a pale cream sheath and a man dressed in a simple gray kilt. Both had long, dark hair that changed colors in a slow cycle. Her soul knew them immediately and she ran to them with a glad sob.

The woman caught Thea in strong, gentle arms and held her as she began to cry. "Shhh, daughter. Be at peace." She sank to the ground and rocked Thea like a child.

After a time Thea's tears eased and she looked up. "He killed my baby, Lady." She wiped her eyes and sat back. "I don't understand and I don't really want to. He hated us so much and we never did anything to him." She sniffled softly through her swollen nose.

Her Lord knelt beside her and stroked her hair. "Your baby is not truly gone, love. It is resting and waiting for another time." He lifted her chin with his fingers. "We are proud of you, daughter. All that pain and terror and you did not curse him. You asked Us to bear witness instead. And We have." He lifted her and cradled her in his lap.

Lady Gaia nodded. "We shall bear witness at his trial."

The three of them were silent for a time. Thea soaked up the comfort and love she felt they were giving her, letting it wash away the stains that Barik's hatred had left.

Eventually Thea lifted her head. "I did not ask the Ta'e'shian Gods to mark me, but I think I understand why they did it now. I would ask your permission, Mother, Father, to be their voice."

Both deities smiled.

"You have Our permission, daughter. But We have things for you to do as well," Skye told her.

Thea nodded and squared her shoulders.

"First," Gaia said, "find your sisters on the ship. There are eight."

"Second," Skye continued in his deep voice, "We will be sending you friendship, recognize it for what it is."

"Third," Gaia spoke again, "face your fears. Do not run and hide from them as We know you want to."

They stood and drew Thea to her feet. Each pressed a kiss to her forehead.

"We must go now, daughter, but remember your husbands love you. Let them help you," Skye said in parting. He brushed his thumb along her cheek.

They left in a cloud of sparkling dust that quickly dissipated in the breeze.

She sat down again as her eyes suddenly grew heavy. A faint rustle in the brush made her turn her head.

A large spotted cat emerged and approached her. She felt no fear as it lightly rubbed its face along her cheek. Turning quickly on its hind feet it darted back into the bushes, and with another rustle, was gone.

Thea was not aware of falling asleep, or of the huge raven watching her from the top of one of the tall pillars.

Heavy moss began to grow thickly under her, forming a soft bed.

The raven glided down from the pillar and landed by the sleeping woman's still form. It tilted its head and studied her carefully with black, gleaming eyes. With a quick shake of its glossy feathers it lifted off the ground and quickly became a black dot in the sky.

Chapter Seventeen

Thea reached out with a trembling hand and stroked the smooth metal casing that held the remains of her child. It was so small, barely the size of her two hands fisted together. Her fingers paused over the etched depressions of her name and her husbands' names. "Robin," she said softly. She turned to the man standing next to her. "My baby is named Robin. Could you please place that name under ours?"

The man nodded solemnly and took the case from her for a moment to carefully etch the words in English. He gave it back to her with a sympathetic look.

It hadn't taken long for word to get around the ship that the captain's mate had been attacked and lost her child as a result. There was much speculation about Barik's actions and what was going to happen to him.

After the artisan left she placed the casket on her bed and checked her appearance once again. Her hair was pulled back into a tight knot. The severe style suited her somber clothing of black slacks and a black turtleneck. She took out a small container of makeup and dabbed a bit of concealing powder on the circles under her eyes.

She took a deep breath and let it out slowly. "I can do this. I *have* to do this." Taking another breath she distanced herself from what she had to do.

She picked up a small, carved, wooden box and placed the casket in the center of it, nestling it into the silk padding the bottom and sides. She closed the lid and walked slowly, purposely to the door.

She made her way steadily to the brig, absently aware of the people moving out of her way. No one tried to stop her. Several people cast sympathetic looks her way, but she didn't notice.

Her husbands weren't aware of what she was doing. She would tell them afterwards, when they couldn't stop her.

She palmed the com on the door, requesting entrance.

People whispered behind her, wondering why she was there, and what she had in the box she was carrying.

The door slid open silently and she stepped inside.

The door closed with a soft hiss and she approached the two security guards sitting at the desk. "I would like to see Barik," she stated quietly, locking her gaze on them.

The guards exchanged nervous glances.

The higher ranking one responded to her. "We don't recommend that, Mistress Theadora."

She inclined her head in acknowledgement of his concern. "Nevertheless, I would like to see him if it is permitted."

He nodded reluctantly. "It's allowed. You will not be able to touch him, or give him any items and the visit will be recorded." He rose and motioned for her to follow him.

She nodded.

He tapped out a code and the door slid open. "Would you like me to stay with you?"

"That would be fine. I will not be long." She followed him into the room and the door shut behind them.

Barik paused in his pacing to glare at her. "What do you want? To gloat?" he snarled at her. His hair lashed angrily around his shoulder like the tail of a furious cat. It was obvious that he hadn't cleaned himself since his arrest. His clothing was rumpled and still stained with her blood.

"No, Barik," she replied quietly. "I wanted to ask you a few questions."

He sneered at her. "What?"

She set down the box and opened it. She carefully withdrew its precious burden and held it up for his view. "I want to know what it feels like to be a murderer."

Barik stared at the casket and paled.

Thea caressed the metal. "I wonder what my baby would have looked like." She turned it to show him the names etched on it. "This is what your hate did. Was it worth it?"

The guard made a strangled sound.

She ignored him.

Barik looked away, schooling his face to blankness.

"Look, damn you!" Thea snarled. Any fear she had felt about facing him again faded as he refused to look at the results of his actions. "This is what it was about, wasn't it? Babies? So, look, and remember!"

His gaze jerked back to her face. She watched him step back from the rage she knew was leaking from her very pores. It would be so easy to hate him, so easy to wish him dead. She wanted to watch him writhe in the karmic pain of his own actions.

"You wanted to hurt us, didn't you? Well, it worked. Those women will never forget you. I will see your face in my dreams for the rest of my life," Thea spat out, letting the fear and pain leach into her voice. "I'm sure your sister is very proud of the legacy you've made for her."

He shook his head, backing up another step. "You'll never replace her." He said it a bit desperately, like a child trying to convince himself that there was no monster under his bed.

She smiled bitterly. "You just don't get it, Barik. We weren't trying to." She turned to the guard. "I'm ready to leave now." She replaced the casket and cradled the box to her chest as she left without a backward glance.

A scream of rage was abruptly cut off as the door slid shut behind them.

The guards stared at her as she quietly thanked them and took her leave.

* * *

Thea made it back to her quarters before she started to shake. She quickly set the case down and sank onto the bed. She'd done it. She'd faced him. Lying down on the bed she curled her knees to her chest.

It wasn't over yet, she knew. There was still the trial, not to mention trying to get past what he'd done. She shuddered.

The door chimed softly. Her com told her it was Sya'tia. "Enter," she said softly, knowing the computer would hear her.

A moment later Sya'tia slipped into the room in her silent way. "Thea?" She sat down on the bed.

Thea patted her friend on the leg. "I'm fine, Sya."

The look on Sya'tia's face said she wasn't so sure of that. "Why did you go to the brig?"

"I had to face him." Thea wasn't surprised her friend had already heard about her visit. She wondered how long it would take her husbands to find out.

"Why?"

"Because he had to see what he had done. And I can't live the rest of my life being afraid," she replied softly.

"Ahhh. I see."

Thea traced the weave of the blanket. "What will the trial be like?" she asked quietly, thinking of the media circuses so common where she was from.

Sya'tia shrugged. "Quiet, I think. The council won't want it to be well known."

Thea sighed and sat up. "Everyone knows. You can see it in their eyes. They watch me." She rubbed her chest where the black cloth of her shirt hid the black bruise that the healing had left behind. Corvin and the healers had managed to reattach the skin Barik had lifted, but the healing of it would be slow. Her mind scrabbled away from the reason she had the bruise.

Sya'tia hugged her friend. "Face them, love. Don't ever turn away."

The smaller woman nodded. She leaned against her friend briefly. "Yeah. I guess so. It's hard to do, though." She stood and tugged Sya'tia into the kitchen. "Corvin is putting me on birth control. He says I should wait at least six months before I try to get pregnant again." She placed a pot of water on the miniature stove and turned on the heat. Her body stiffened as another low cramp rolled through her. "God, I hope these cramps stop soon."

Sya'tia nodded sympathetically.

The door chimed softly.

"That's probably Corvin again. He's been checking on me every couple of hours. Come in." She took out a plate of cookies.

Sya'tia took out cups and placed them on the counter.

Kati darted into the room and hugged a surprised Thea. "Thea! I'm so sorry!" The young woman hugged Thea again and stepped back.

Soren slid into the room. "Hi, Thea." He bit his lip. "We wanted to come see you in medical but thought you might want to rest, so we came today, since you were home."

Thea hugged her friend tightly. "Thank you for coming over. Would you like to have cookies and tea with us? Do you know Sya'tia?"

Both of them nodded and smiled shyly at the tall woman.

Sya'tia returned their greetings and got another cup. She shooed Thea into a chair. "I can get it, you're starting to look pale again, love."

Soren sat in a chair with a thump. "Thea, the asana asked me to give you their condolences. Many of them wanted to come, but they didn't want to intrude either."

She nodded tiredly. "Tell them thank you for me, please." She smiled gratefully up at Sya'tia when she set a cup of tea in front of her and the plate of cookies in the center of the table.

"Father wanted to come, too," Kati chimed in. "So did my other parents." She picked up a cookie and sniffed it curiously. She nibbled the edge. "Mmm these are good!" She took a big bite, trying to chew and smile at the same time.

Sya'tia sat down with her own cup after serving Soren and Kati theirs.

* * *

Kyrin arrived at the science offices to meet Daeshen and walk home with him, as was their custom. His husband quickly finished putting his desk to rights and they walked down the hall.

After a bit of silence Kyrin spoke. "Barik goes into stasis tomorrow morning."

Daeshen nodded.

They quickly arrived at their quarters and entered. Both men were surprised by the sound of Thea laughing softly.

Daeshen's eyes lightened at the sound.

They went to see what was amusing her. They found Thea sitting at the table laughing while Soren tried to knock Sya'tia down with a movement he had seen in a human movie.

She rapidly blocked the move and tripped the young man.

Thea giggled again as Sya'tia helped him up and offered to give him a bit more training in hand to hand fighting.

Kati was standing behind Thea, brushing her hair with an enthralled expression, chattering a mile a minute about hairstyles she wanted to try putting the thick mass in.

Both men smiled, watching the scene.

Kyrin said, "Hey, can we join the party?" and strode toward his wife for a kiss.

Daeshen slipped over and hugged Sya'tia and Soren. "Thank you for coming. It means a lot to her, I can feel it."

Soren shrugged bashfully. "She's our friend," he said simply.

Sya'tia smiled and relaxed easily against him. "You don't have to thank us for caring about her, Daeshen. It's easy to do." She watched Kyrin tease Kati about her fascination with human hair.

The door chimed again.

Thea rolled her eyes. "Come in." It seemed their quarters were going to be Grand Central Station tonight. "Guess I should have the galley send dinner, I don't feel like cooking tonight," she murmured to her husband.

He smiled. "I'll handle it, love."

Corvin entered the dining room and smiled at all the people gathered there. "Well, I see you've got plenty of people to keep you company." He set down a covered tray. "Shana sent you some 'comfort food' and said to tell you to keep your chin up. Whatever that means."

Thea smiled wanly. "Thanks, Corvin." She took the cover off the tray. "Oh, how sweet. She sent an ice cream pizza. We can have this after dinner. You're all staying aren't you?"

There was a chorus of agreement.

Kyrin rolled his eyes and commed the galley back and requested triple the amount of food he'd just ordered.

The evening passed quickly, but Thea was exhausted by the time she said goodnight to their last guest. She made her way back to the bedroom and began removing her clothes.

Daeshen joined her after a moment and he looked at the box curiously. "What's this?" Kyrin came in just as he was opening it. "Oh…" Daeshen's voice trailed off as he looked at the tiny egg-like casket. She saw his eyes fill with tears. "You named him. What does it mean?" His hands caressed the cool metal.

Thea swallowed hard, feeling her grief over her lost child again. "Robin. It's one of the first birds to come back in the spring. They are beautiful." She leaned against Kyrin's chest.

He hugged her tightly, tears burning his eyes. "Close the lid, Daeshen. Let's go to bed. We'll take Robin to the stasis hold tomorrow." Their baby would not be buried until they reached Ta'e.

He tenderly put both of his mates to bed before crawling in with them. He curled himself close to Thea and put his arm around them both.

Thea looked at the faces of her husbands. "I want to ask Sya'tia to marry us. But, not yet, it's too soon and I think she should be courted properly. Do either of you mind?"

Daeshen shook his head sleepily. "Not at all, love, I think she should be courted as well and I would welcome her in our home."

Kyrin murmured a soft agreement. His arms tightened around them. He shook inwardly as he thought of how close he had come to losing Thea. His eyes burned as he thought of the child they had lost. While he wanted Sya'tia to join them because he cared for her he also wanted the added protection for his family. He felt Daeshen relax and heard his breathing deepen and felt himself relax as well. Soon, his mind blurred and he was asleep.

Thea sighed deeply and drifted off to sleep, finally feeling safe again, cradled between them both. "I love you," she whispered inaudibly to their sleeping forms.

Epilogue

Skye and Gaia looked down at the eighteen pairs of eyes watching them intently.

"Your mission, should you choose to accept it..." Skye intoned in a solemn tone, belied by the twinkle in his eye. "Is to confound, harass and generally annoy the enemy to the point that they are gibbering monkeys"

Gaia laughed. "Thank you for volunteering. Have each of you picked a partner and a Mistress?" She inspected them with satisfaction. Each of the volunteers was intelligent and at the end of their respective rebirth cycles and able to choose where they wanted to go.

All of them nodded, crafty, evil gleams of mischief in their eyes. Each of them was looking forward to this new adventure and the prize that awaited them at the end.

Skye sat down in the easy chair that materialized behind him. "Just remember, go to your Mistress if you get into trouble. Use your gifts wisely, children. And no fighting."

Gaia kissed each of them and then both Gods sent them to the ship. "Let the next act in their play commence... With a few surprises." She smirked.

Skye snickered in his chair.

~ * ~

Glossary of Terms

Arkaa -- planet where samples are to be collected

Arkaana -- ace of humanoid spider people

Asana -- Priest(s) and Priestess(es) of the Lithen; group term

Byasuen -- Goddess of Craft and Arts (Ta'e)

Cerebcom -- technology implanted in the brain to allow communication between a ship's artificial intelligence and/or another individual who also has an implant

Chosen -- individual of Ta'e'shian society who is born with markings showing they are favored by the Gods

Com -- to send a communication to someone using an implanted cerebcom

Corgan -- motorized object used to pull someone through water at high speed

Creamstal -- powdered shell of a sea snail, used in cooking

Crystalshroom -- type of mushroom that secretes a liquid that hardens upon contact with air, used in artwork

Chrystarea -- sea flower, blooms once every seven years

Deema -- affectionate term for "father"

Dorya -- small fish that travel in large school, also known as nibblers

Ecoha -- God of Craft and Arts (Ta'e)

Felbos -- messy sea creature; similar to a monkey

Gaia -- generic name used to refer to Lady of Witches (Goddess)

God-marks -- features used to identify Chosen of the Gods

Holoreader -- a small flat computer used in place of paper

Iliria -- Goddess of Healing (Ta'e)

Kashka -- Goddess of Warriors (Ta'e)

Kyen -- Gentleman, or gentlemen

Kysout -- God of Soul Renewal (Ta'e)

Lavoya -- dinner dish made with seafood, dish title, not an ingredient

Lith -- single set of Gods and Goddesses of the Ta'e'sha

Lithen -- Gods and Goddesses of the Ta'e'sha as a whole group

Meecha -- animal native to Ta'e

Mo'aton -- God of Healing (Ta'e)

Samonan -- Goddess of Soul Renewal (Ta'e)

Saras -- shape shift; to change one's form

Sea Fern -- food plant, grown and used similarly to wheat

Sha'ki -- moon of Shya, to be terraformed

Shaysha -- Goddess of Spiritual Balance and Mental Healing (Ta'e)

Sho'bi -- moon of Shya, to be terraformed

Shoomoe -- dinner dish of fish fillets and fried vegetables

Shya -- planet to be terraformed

Skye -- generic name used to refer to Lord of Witches (God)

Solune -- God of Spiritual Balance and Mental Healing (Ta'e)

Sparker -- wire suit, used as a sex toy

Tabet -- Goddess of Atlantis

Teirnan -- God of Atlantis

Vosh -- God of Warriors (Ta'e)

THE END

Theolyn Boese

Theolyn Boese lives in Oregon with her wide assortment of animals, which include two cats, Goblyn and Stupid (yes that really is his name and well earned), a Border Collie named Fuzzbutt, a few ducks, and her pheasant, Samurai.

She has been writing since grade school, staring with a poetry class her teacher enrolled her in to help her learn to work with dyslexia. Bolstered by her teacher's faith in her she quickly learned to love reading and writing instead of being afraid of it. Soon after she was reading voraciously and scribbling poems on everything.

She would love to hear from her readers and invites them to write to her at Sabrielle@gmail.com, and to check out her website at http://www.theolynboese.com.

ANTHOLOGIES AVAILABLE In Print from Loose Id®

HARD CANDY
Angela Knight, Sheri Gilmore & Morgan Hawke

HOWL
Jet Mykles, Raine Weaver & Jeigh Lynn

RATED: X-MAS
Rachel Bo, Barbara Karmazin & Jet Mykles

ROMANCE AT THE EDGE: IN OTHER WORLDS
MaryJanice Davidson, Angela Knight & Camille Anthony

THE BITE BEORE CHRISTMAS
Laura Baumbach, Sedonia Guillone & Kit Tunstall

WILD WISHES
Stephanie Burke, Lena Matthews & Eve Vaughn

Publisher's Note: The print titles listed above were previously released in e-book format by Loose Id®.

Non-fiction from Loose Id®

PASSIONATE INK
ANGELA KNIGHT

OTHER TITLES AVAILABLE In Print from Loose Id®

ALPHA
Treva Harte

COURTESAN
Louisa Trent

DANGEROUS CRAVINGS
Evangeline Anderson

DINAH'S DARK DESIRE
Mechele Armstrong

HEAVEN SENT: HELL & PURGATORY
Jet Mykles

HEAVEN SENT 2
Jet Mykles

LEASHED: MORE THAN A BARGAIN
Jet Mykles

INTERSTELLAR SERVICE & DISCIPLINE: VICTORIOUS STAR
Morgan Hawke

THE TIN STAR

J. L. Langley

STRENGTH IN NUMBERS

Rachel Bo

THE TIN STAR

J. L. Langley

THE BROKEN H

J. L. Langley

THE COMPLETENESS OF CELIA FLYNN

Sedonia Guillone

THE PRENDARIAN CHRONICLES

Doreen DeSalvo

THE SYNDICATE: VOLUMES 1 & 2

Jules Jones & Alex Woolgrave

VIRTUAL MURDER

Jennifer Macaire

WHY ME?

Treva Harte

Publisher's Note: The print titles listed above were previously released in e-book format by Loose Id®.